MURDER IN PARIS

HAZEL CHASE MYSTERIES
BOOK 1

ARTHUR PEARCE

Copyright © 2025 Arthur Pearce

All rights reserved.

No part of this book may be reproduced, distributed, or transmitted in any form or by any means, including photocopying, recording, or other electronic or mechanical methods, without the prior written permission of the author, except in the case of brief quotations embodied in critical reviews and certain other noncommercial uses permitted by copyright law. For permission requests, please contact the author.

"Murder in Paris" is a work of fiction. Names, characters, businesses, places, events and incidents either are products of the author's imagination or are used fictitiously. Any resemblance to actual persons, living or dead, events, or locales is entirely coincidental.

ISBN: 979-8-2978-1184-3

1

"Wow, is that Paris?"

Hazel pressed her face against the airplane window, her breath fogging the glass. Below, the city sprawled like a constellation fallen to earth. Thousands of lights winked and shimmered in the darkness, tracing the curves of the Seine as it wound through the heart of the city.

The Eiffel Tower stood out like a golden beacon, its spotlight sweeping across the midnight sky. Streets radiated outward in geometric patterns broken by the organic sprawl of older neighborhoods. Even from ten thousand feet, Paris looked exactly like she'd imagined—magical, mysterious, alive.

She fumbled for her phone, trying to capture the view through the window. The photos came out mostly as blurry lights and her own reflection, but she didn't care. She was actually here. Actually doing this.

"First time?"

The voice startled her. The woman in the middle seat had been asleep for most of the eleven-hour flight from Los Angeles, or at least buried in a paperback romance novel with a shirtless man on the cover. Hazel had assumed she wasn't the chatty type.

The woman looked to be in her mid-fifties, with silver-streaked auburn hair pulled back in an elegant twist. She wore a cream-colored blazer over dark jeans, a silk scarf draped artfully around her neck. Everything about her screamed effortless French chic, though when she spoke again, her accent was unmistakably American with just a hint of French inflection.

"Your first time in Paris, I mean," the woman clarified, smiling. "I could tell from the gasps and the hundred photos you've been taking through the window. My daughter does the same thing whenever we fly somewhere new. She must have taken a thousand pictures of London from the air last summer."

Heat crept up Hazel's neck. She hadn't realized she'd been that obvious. "Actually, it's my first time anywhere. I mean, outside California. First time on a plane, too."

"Ah." The woman's smile widened, kind rather than condescending. "That explains the death grip on the armrest during takeoff."

Hazel laughed, remembering her panic as the plane had accelerated down the runway. She'd spent the entire wait in the terminal reading articles about aviation disasters on her phone—not her smartest move. When the engines had roared to life, she'd been convinced they were all about to become another statistic.

"I may have overreacted a tiny bit," she admitted.

"We all have our moments." The woman marked her place in her book with a boarding pass. "On my first flight, I was convinced the wings were going to fall off. I kept watching them flex during turbulence and thinking, 'Metal isn't supposed to bend like that.'"

"Wait, they're supposed to flex?" Hazel's eyes widened.

The woman laughed. "Oh dear, I shouldn't have said that. Yes, perfectly normal. Engineering marvel, actually." She shifted in her seat, turning to face Hazel more fully. "So what brings you to Paris? Visiting someone? Vacation?"

"Neither, actually." Hazel turned back to the window, watching the city grow larger as they descended.

She opened her mouth to explain, then closed it again.

The story was too long, too complicated for a stranger on a plane.

2

It had all really started twenty-three years ago, though Hazel had only learned the important parts three months back.

Her parents had died when she was two—a car accident. Hazel's memories of them were more like impressions: her mother's laugh, her father's cologne, a feeling of being held. Nothing concrete. Nothing real.

Her grandmother had raised her. Bridget Chase had been a small woman with steel in her spine and opinions about everything. They'd lived in a two-bedroom house in Fillmore, close enough to Los Angeles to feel its influence but far enough away to maintain that small-town feel.

Bridget worked as a seamstress, taking in alterations and custom orders from her converted garage workshop. They'd never been poor exactly, but money was always tight. Vacations meant driving to Malibu for the day. New clothes came from the Goodwill in Ventura.

"You don't need to go gallivanting around the world," Bridget would say whenever Hazel mentioned wanting to travel. "Everything you need is right here. That's what's wrong with people today—always looking for something better instead of appreciating what they have."

College had been out of the question. Not just because of money—though that was part of it—but because Bridget couldn't bear the thought of Hazel leaving. "You want to abandon me like everyone else?" she'd say, and Hazel would feel that familiar twist of guilt in her stomach.

So Hazel had stayed. After high school, she'd gotten a job at Sunrise Bakery on Central Avenue. It wasn't a bad life. She liked her coworkers, loved the smell of fresh bread in the morning, found satisfaction in creating something people enjoyed. She'd learned to bake from her grandmother—one of the few activities they'd genuinely enjoyed together—and she was good at it. Really good, actually. Customers started requesting her croissants specifically. Her lemon tarts sold out every weekend.

Days turned into weeks, weeks into years. Hazel developed a routine: up at 4 AM, walk to the bakery, prep the day's pastries, serve customers with a smile, home by 4 PM. Dinner with Grandma. Maybe a movie on Netflix. Bed by 9. Repeat.

She'd dated a few guys from town. Nothing serious. Tommy Park from high school had taken her to prom and they'd tried to make it work for a while after, but he'd wanted to move to San Francisco for college and she'd had to stay. There'd been others—the mechanic who fixed her ancient Honda, a customer who came in every morning for a bear claw and black coffee—but nothing that made her want to upend her quiet life.

Then, three months ago, Bridget had died. Heart attack in her sleep. Peaceful, the doctor said, as if that somehow made it better.

Hazel had found her that morning when she'd gone to wake her for breakfast. The house had felt different the moment she'd walked into the bedroom—too still, too quiet. Bridget looked smaller somehow, like death had diminished her.

The funeral was modest. Bridget hadn't had many friends, and most of the family was long gone. Hazel stood at the graveside in her one black dress, accepting condolences from people, feeling untethered. For twenty-three years, her life had revolved around her grandmother. Now what?

She'd taken a leave from the bakery. "Take all the time you need," her coworker Janet had said, pulling her into a flour-scented hug.

Then came the meeting with Mr. Pemberton, her grandmother's lawyer. He'd called three days after the funeral, his voice gentle but insistent. "There are some matters regarding your grandmother's estate that we need to discuss."

Hazel had assumed he meant the house, maybe a small life insurance policy. She'd sat in his mahogany-paneled office, staring at his collection of dusty law books, completely unprepared for what came next.

"Your grandmother was quite a wealthy woman," he'd said, sliding a folder across his desk.

Hazel had almost laughed. Bridget, who'd darned her socks until they had more patches than original fabric? Bridget, who'd repaired her reading glasses with tape rather than buy new ones? Bridget, who'd saved aluminum cans to take to the recycling center for the five-cent deposits?

"There must be some mistake."

"No mistake." Mr. Pemberton adjusted his wire-rimmed glasses. "Your parents, before their death, transferred a substantial sum to your grandmother's account. It appears they did this just days before the accident."

"How much?"

When he told her, Hazel had to ask him to repeat it. Twice.

"But... where did my parents get that kind of money?"

Mr. Pemberton spread his hands. "I'm afraid I don't know. The records only show the transfer, not its origin. What I can tell you is that your grandmother never touched the principal. She lived off her seamstress income and let the money sit, accumulating interest. Twenty-three years of compound interest on that amount... well, you can see the results."

Hazel stared at the numbers until they blurred. "She never spent any of it?"

"There were a few small withdrawals over the years. Medical expenses, a new roof in 2018, your car repairs last year. But nothing substantial. It's all documented here." He tapped another folder. "Your grandmother left very specific instructions. Everything goes to you."

Hazel had left the office in a daze. All those years of scrimping and saving, of missing school trips because they couldn't afford them, of Bridget shopping with coupons and buying day-old bread, and she'd been sitting on a fortune. Why? What was the point of having money if you never used it?

But anger gave way to possibility. For the first time in her life, Hazel could do whatever she wanted. Travel. Go to college. Buy a car made in this century. Hell, buy ten cars.

Instead, she'd found herself in her kitchen one evening, kneading dough and thinking. This was what she knew. This was what she was good at. But maybe... maybe she could do it on her own terms.

The idea of her own bakery had always been a dream, something for "someday." Now someday had arrived with a bank account to match.

But if she was going to compete, really compete, she needed to be better. She needed to learn from the best.

Which was how she'd found herself on the website for L'Académie de la Pâtisserie Française at 2 AM, credit card in hand.

"I'm here for pastry school," Hazel told the woman on the plane, leaving out the family drama and existential crisis. "Two-week intensive course at L'Académie de la…" She paused, struggling with the pronunciation. "L'Académie de la Pâtiss—"

"Pâtisserie Française?" The woman's eyebrows rose. "Well, then we'll be seeing quite a bit of each other. Eleanor Moore." She extended a manicured hand. "I'm the deputy director. I also assist with the classes."

Hazel's stomach dropped. Of course. Of course the one person she'd actually talked to on this flight would turn out to be part of the school staff. She shook Eleanor's hand, trying to look more put-together than she felt in her wrinkled t-shirt and travel-worn jeans.

"Hazel Chase. I, uh, I think I saw your photo on the website."

"Probably the one from five years ago. I keep meaning to update it." Eleanor's smile was warm. "How wonderful that we happened to be on the same flight. I was visiting my sister in Los Angeles—she just had her third baby. Can you imagine? At forty-two?"

"Wow," Hazel said, because she couldn't think of anything else.

"I know. I told her she was crazy, but she's always done things her own way." Eleanor's accent became more pronounced when she was animated. "I've been living in France since I was fifteen. My parents moved us there for my father's work—he was with the State Department. I fell in love with Paris and never left."

"And you got into baking there?"

"Oh, that's a story." Eleanor laughed. "I was supposed to be pre-law at the Sorbonne. Very serious, very ambitious. My father had my whole life mapped out—law school, State Department, follow in his footsteps. Then I took a part-time job at a patisserie to improve my French, and... well. There's something about creating something beautiful that people can enjoy, isn't there? My parents were horrified when I dropped out to attend culinary school."

"But it worked out."

"Eventually. Charles—Charles Lambert, the director—he took a chance on me when I had almost no experience. We've built something special at L'Académie." Eleanor's eyes sparkled with pride. "You're going to love it. Small class sizes, hands-on instruction, and the guest chef this session is extraordinary."

"Who is it?"

"Now that would be telling." Eleanor winked. "But trust me, you won't be disappointed."

The plane shuddered slightly as they hit a pocket of turbulence. Hazel's knuckles went white on the armrest.

"Just a little bump," Eleanor said gently. "We're starting our descent. Look at me, not out the window. That's it. Deep breath. You know what the worst part of turbulence is?"

"Dying?" Hazel suggested.

Eleanor laughed. "Spilling your wine. I once ruined a silk blouse during turbulence over the Atlantic."

Hazel pressed her face to the window again, watching Paris grow closer, larger, more real with every passing second.

"I can't believe I'm actually here," she said, mostly to herself.

"Believe it. And just wait until you see the city in daylight. There's nothing quite like your first morning in Paris. Though

August can be tricky—half the city is on vacation. But that means shorter lines at the tourist spots, so really, you've timed it perfectly."

The pilot's voice crackled over the intercom, first in French, then in accented English, announcing their final approach. The ground rushed up to meet them, and then—with a bump that made Hazel's stomach lurch—they were down.

Half the plane burst into applause. Hazel joined in enthusiastically, clapping until her palms stung. She was here. She was actually in Paris. She'd survived her first flight.

Eleanor rolled her eyes good-naturedly. "First-time flyers," she murmured, but she was smiling. "Though I suppose for your maiden voyage, some celebration is warranted."

"I'm never doing that again," Hazel said, then immediately reconsidered. "I mean, I have to fly home, don't I? Oh god."

3

"Share a ride?" Eleanor suggested as they waited for their luggage at the carousel. "I live on-site during the courses—one of the perks of being deputy director. The school sends a driver for me. Plenty of room in the car."

Hazel hefted her oversized suitcase off the belt. She'd definitely overpacked, cramming in everything from formal dresses (what if there was a fancy dinner?) to rain boots (she'd heard it rained a lot in Paris). "That would be great, actually. I wasn't sure how I was going to get there."

The driver was waiting just outside customs, holding a small sign that read "Moore." He was tall and thin, with a magnificent mustache and the put-upon expression of someone who'd been waiting too long. He said something rapid in French to Eleanor, who responded in kind.

"Jean-Paul, this is Hazel Chase, one of our new students. Hazel, Jean-Paul has been driving for the school for... how long now?"

"Quinze ans, madame." He took Hazel's suitcase without asking, hefting it like it weighed nothing.

"Fifteen years," Eleanor translated. "He knows every shortcut in Paris. Also every good restaurant, every traffic pattern, and the personal gossip of half the city. Isn't that right, Jean-Paul?"

"I know nothing," Jean-Paul said in heavily accented English. "I am like the tomb."

"Like the tomb that told me about the minister's affair last month?"

"That was public service," Jean-Paul protested. "The people have a right to know."

Hazel attempted a "Bonjour, Jean-Paul," but must have mangled it badly because he winced slightly before responding with a stream of French she couldn't follow.

"He says welcome to Paris," Eleanor said diplomatically.

The car was a black Mercedes, spotlessly clean despite the light rain that had started falling. Hazel slid into the back seat, Eleanor beside her, and pressed her face to the window like a child. Paris at night was even more magical from ground level. The buildings glowed golden in the streetlights, their shuttered windows and wrought-iron balconies straight from a movie set. Cafés spilled onto sidewalks despite the late hour, people huddled under awnings with wine and cigarettes. A couple kissed passionately on a street corner, oblivious to the rain.

"It's exactly like I pictured," Hazel breathed. "Like a movie."

"Just wait until you smell the metro in August," Jean-Paul called from the front seat. "Very authentic, not like movie at all."

"Jean-Paul, don't ruin the magic," Eleanor scolded. "She'll have plenty of time to discover Paris's less charming qualities."

"What qualities? Paris has no bad qualities. Except the tourists. And the prices. And the—"

"The driving," Eleanor interrupted. "Speaking of which, eyes on the road, please."

Jean-Paul muttered something in French and swerved around a delivery truck parked in the middle of the lane.

They drove in comfortable silence for a while, Hazel taking in every detail—the way the street lamps reflected on the wet cobblestones, the glimpses of the Seine between buildings, the occasional burst of music from an open door. Her exhaustion was battling with excitement, and excitement was winning.

"Almost there now," Eleanor said, looking up from her phone. "I hope Charles is still awake. He texted earlier that he wanted to greet all the new students personally, but that was hours ago."

"What's he like? Charles?"

"Brilliant. Demanding. A perfectionist, but in the best way." Eleanor was texting again, thumbs flying. "He built L'Académie from nothing. Started with one room and a broken oven, now we're one of the most respected pastry schools in the world."

They'd left the bustling streets behind, turning onto quieter roads lined with enormous houses set back behind high walls. The rain had picked up, drumming on the car roof. The windshield wipers beat a hypnotic rhythm.

"We're in the 16th arrondissement now," Eleanor explained. "Very upscale, very quiet. The school is in the Villa Montmorency—it's a private community within Paris. Gated, guarded, very secure. The school acquired the property about fifteen years ago."

"How does a pastry school afford a place like that?"

"Our fees help," Eleanor said with a wry smile. "But also, Charles is very good at finding sponsors. Plus, we host private events, corporate team-building, that sort of thing."

The car slowed as they approached an actual gatehouse, complete with a security barrier and uniformed guard. It looked more like the entrance to a military base than a neighborhood. The guard emerged from his booth, flashlight in hand despite the streetlights.

Eleanor rolled down her window and spoke to the guard in French. He bent to peer into the back seat, his gaze landing on Hazel. He checked something on his clipboard, asked Eleanor another question, then nodded and returned to his booth.

"Bon retour, Madame Moore," he said as the barrier rose. Then, switching to accented but clear English: "And welcome to Paris, Mademoiselle Chase. I hope you enjoy your stay with us."

"Thank you," Hazel managed, wondering how he knew her name.

"They have a list," Eleanor explained as they drove through. "Security is tight here. Too many high-profile residents. You'll get used to it."

The Villa Montmorency was like stepping into another world. The houses here weren't just big—they were estates, each one unique, surrounded by manicured gardens and tall hedges that provided privacy. Gas lamps—actual gas lamps—lined the streets, casting everything in a warm, romantic glow.

"This is insane," Hazel muttered. "People actually live here?"

"Oh yes. That house there?" Eleanor pointed to a particularly grand mansion. "Saudi prince. And that one belongs to the CEO of one of the big luxury brands. I forget which one. Charles knows them all, of course. He's very good at being neighborly when it suits the school's interests."

"And they don't mind having a school here?"

"We're very discreet. Small classes, no parties. Well, no loud parties. And Charles makes sure to invite the neighbors to our special events. Nothing like free champagne and canapés to maintain good relations."

The car pulled into a circular driveway. The building that housed L'Académie de la Pâtisserie Française was a three-story villa in cream-colored stone, with tall windows and delicate ironwork balconies. Ivy climbed one wall, and the front door—massive, wooden, probably older than Hazel's entire hometown—stood open, spilling warm light onto the rain-slicked cobblestones.

"Home sweet home," Eleanor said. "Ah, look, Charles is waiting for us."

Two figures emerged as the car stopped. The first was a tiny woman in a black dress and sensible shoes, her gray hair pulled back in a tight bun. She moved with the quick efficiency of someone used to being busy.

The second was a man in his fifties, tall and distinguished, with silver hair and the kind of posture that suggested military service or ballet training. He wore pressed khakis and a button-down shirt despite the late hour.

"Eleanor, welcome back." His English was accented but precise. "How was Los Angeles? How is your sister?"

"Exhausted but happy. Three children, Charles. I told her she's lost her mind."

"Children are a blessing," he said automatically, then turned to Hazel. "And this must be..."

He stopped mid-sentence, staring at Hazel as she climbed out of the car. The color drained from his face. For a moment, he looked like he'd seen a ghost.

"Mademoiselle Chase," he finished, recovering quickly. The professional smile snapped back into place, but Hazel had seen that flash of... what? Recognition? Fear? "Welcome to L'Académie. I'm Charles Lambert, the director."

"Nice to meet you." Hazel shook his offered hand, noting that his palm was slightly damp.

"Madame Dubois will show you to your room." He gestured to the small woman, who was already wrestling Hazel's suitcase from Jean-Paul. "The other students have already arrived and are settling in. Breakfast will be delivered to your room at eight, and your first class begins at nine in the demonstration kitchen."

"Let me help with that," Hazel said, reaching for her suitcase.

Madame Dubois waved her off. "Non, non. You are guest." Her English was heavily accented but determined. She lifted the suitcase with surprising ease for someone who couldn't weigh more than ninety pounds.

"I'll see you tomorrow," Eleanor told Hazel. "Sleep well."

"Thank you for everything," Hazel said. "The ride, the company... I really appreciate it."

Hazel followed Madame Dubois into the villa, trying not to gawk. The entrance hall alone was bigger than her grandmother's entire house. A chandelier that belonged in a museum hung from the coffered ceiling. The floors were polished marble, the walls covered in what looked like original oil paintings. A grand staircase curved up to the second floor, its banister gleaming with centuries of polish.

"Your room, troisième étage," Madame Dubois said, already halfway up the stairs despite the heavy suitcase.

The third floor. Hazel hurried to keep up, her sneakers squeaking on the marble. They passed closed doors with brass numbers, the hallway lit by sconces that looked like they'd once held candles. Everything smelled faintly of lavender and old wood.

"Voilà." Madame Dubois stopped at a door marked 7 and produced an old-fashioned key. "Your room."

Hazel stepped inside and bit back a gasp. The room was enormous, with tall windows overlooking the garden, a four-poster bed with gauzy curtains, and an antique writing desk. The bathroom, glimpsed through an open door, had a clawfoot tub and marble countertops.

"Is okay?" Madame Dubois asked, setting the suitcase on a luggage rack.

"It's perfect. Absolutely perfect."

The housekeeper showed her how to work the radiator, pointed out extra blankets in the armoire, demonstrated the quirky lock on the bathroom door. "Breakfast, eight o'clock, I bring here."

"Yes, thank you. Merci."

"Bon." Madame Dubois paused at the door. "You need anything, you ring." She pointed to an actual bell pull by the bed. "Bonne nuit, mademoiselle."

And then Hazel was alone.

She sank onto the bed—ridiculously soft, with sheets that felt like silk—and tried to process the last twenty-four hours. This morning, she'd woken up in her childhood bedroom in Fillmore, surrounded by stuffed animals and participation trophies. Now she was in a mansion in Paris, about to learn from a world-class pastry chef.

Her phone buzzed. International roaming had kicked in. A text from Janet at the bakery: *Hope you landed safe! Send pictures!*

Hazel walked to the window, pushing aside heavy curtains. The garden below was lit by subtle landscape lighting, revealing neat paths between shaped hedges. In the distance, lights twinkled from other villas.

But as exhaustion finally caught up with her—it was still afternoon in California, but her body was confused—one thing nagged at her mind.

Charles Lambert's face when he'd seen her. That moment of shock, quickly hidden but definitely there.

Did he know her somehow?

Hazel shook her head, trying to dislodge the thought. She was being paranoid. She had one of those faces, that was all. Generic American girl, nothing special. He'd probably just been surprised by how young she looked or something equally mundane.

Still, as she got ready for bed, splashing water on her travel-worn face and changing into pajamas that seemed too casual for the elegant room, she couldn't shake the feeling that Charles Lambert had recognized her.

But from where?

4

Hazel woke to complete darkness and a moment of pure panic. Where was she? The bed was too soft, the air smelled wrong—lavender instead of the vanilla candle she always burned at home. Then memory crashed back: Paris. The villa. Pastry school.

She fumbled for her phone on the unfamiliar nightstand. 3:47 AM. Her body thought it was dinner time in California, and her stomach agreed. She'd been too nervous to eat much on the plane, surviving on airline pretzels and half a rubbery chicken breast.

Sleep was clearly done with her. She padded to the window and pushed aside the heavy curtains. The garden below was dark except for subtle uplighting on a few trees. Paris was out there somewhere, but from here she could have been anywhere.

Her stomach growled again. Loudly.

"Shut up," she told it. "Breakfast is in—" She checked her phone. "Four hours."

Four hours. She could do this. She'd just... what? Unpack? Read? Count sheep in French? She didn't even know the word for sheep.

By the time soft knocking came at 8 AM sharp, Hazel had unpacked everything twice, arranged and rearranged her toiletries in the marble bathroom, taken approximately forty-seven photos of the room to send to Janet, and read the entire student information packet three times. She knew the fire exit locations, the Wi-Fi password, and that students were "kindly requested to refrain from intimate relations on school premises." That last bit had made her snort. Who came to pastry school to hook up?

"Entrez!" she called, attempting the French phrase she'd been practicing since 4 AM. It probably came out sounding more like "on-tray," but at least she'd tried.

Madame Dubois bustled in with a tray that looked heavier than she was. The smell hit Hazel first—butter, coffee, something sweet and yeasted. Her stomach, which had been complaining for hours, practically sang hallelujahs.

"Bonjour, mademoiselle. You sleep well?"

"Yes, very well," Hazel lied. No point in explaining jet lag to someone who probably hadn't left France in decades.

Madame Dubois set the tray on the small table by the window. "I bring traditional breakfast. Croissant, pain au chocolat, confiture—jam, yes? Orange juice fresh. Coffee strong."

"This is traditional?" Hazel stared at the spread. The croissant alone was the size of her hand, golden and flaky and perfect. The jam came in three tiny pots—strawberry, apricot, and something purple she couldn't identify. The coffee smelled like heaven had been distilled into liquid form.

"Oui. Eat all, you need energy. First day, the chef, he work you hard." Madame Dubois mimed aggressive stirring. "Also, nine o'clock, you come to hall. Madame Moore, she collect everyone, take to kitchen."

"I'll be there."

"Bon." The housekeeper headed for the door, then paused. "The clothes, mademoiselle. You bring apron?"

"Apron?" Hazel's stomach dropped. Of course she needed an apron. Why hadn't she thought of that? "I don't—"

"No worry. We have aprons. Beautiful ones, with school logo." Madame Dubois's eyes twinkled with amusement. "For the price you pay, we give you moon if you ask for it, yes?"

With that, she left, and Hazel found herself smiling. So even the stern housekeeper had a sense of humor.

Hazel attacked the breakfast with American enthusiasm and zero French elegance. The croissant shattered at first bite, sending flakes cascading onto the pristine white tablecloth. The coffee was strong enough to wake the dead—or at least the severely jet-lagged. She tried the purple jam (plum, maybe?) and nearly moaned. Everything tasted better here. Even the butter seemed more buttery, if that was possible.

By 8:40 she was showered, dressed in her most practical outfit—jeans, sneakers, and a black t-shirt that wouldn't show flour too badly—and attempting to tame her hair into something resembling professional. She'd brought minimal makeup. This was pastry school, not a fashion show.

The entrance hall looked even more impressive in daylight. Morning sun streamed through tall windows, making the chandelier crystals throw rainbows across the marble floor. Six women stood in a loose cluster near the door, their voices echoing in the vast space.

Hazel's first thought was that she'd somehow signed up for the wrong course. These weren't students—they were ladies who lunched. Three of them looked ready for a charity gala, not a kitchen. Perfect makeup, designer clothes, heels that would be a liability around hot stoves. The woman closest to Hazel wore a white silk blouse that probably cost more than Hazel's old car. Who wore white silk to cook?

The other three had at least dressed practically, though even their "casual" looked expensive. Quality fabrics, well-fitted, the kind of effortless style that actually took enormous effort.

They all looked older than her. Thirties at least, some maybe forties. Sophisticated. Worldly. Everything Hazel wasn't.

"Hazel!" Eleanor appeared from a side door, today in crisp chef's whites that somehow looked chic rather than utilitarian. "Perfect timing. Come meet everyone."

The introductions blurred together. Isabella Giuliani from Italy, the one in the white silk, with diamond earrings that caught the light. Sofia Andersson from Sweden, tall and blonde and intimidatingly beautiful. Monique Beaumont, French, with the kind of perfectly tousled hair that Hazel had tried and failed to achieve that morning.

The practical dressers were Priya Patel from London, who had a firm handshake and shrewd eyes; Yuki Tanaka from Tokyo, petite and serious-looking; and Xu Fei from Beijing, who smiled warmly and said "Nice to meet you" in carefully pronounced English.

"We're just waiting for one more," Eleanor said, checking her phone. "He should be—"

She glanced toward the staircase. "Ah, here he is now."

A man was descending the stairs, and Hazel's brain short-circuited.

5

The man was tall—maybe six-two—with the kind of bone structure that made photographers weep with joy. Dark hair, artfully tousled (did everyone in France wake up with perfect hair?), and eyes the color of good whiskey. He wore jeans and a white button-down with the sleeves rolled up, managing to look both casual and put-together. He moved with the easy confidence of someone who'd never met a room he couldn't charm.

He said something in French to Eleanor, who laughed and responded in kind. Great. Another person who'd make Hazel feel like a monolingual American idiot.

"Everyone, this is Louis Bassett," Eleanor said, switching to English. "Our final student. Louis, meet your classmates."

His eyes swept the group and landed on Hazel. Something flickered across his face—interest? Amusement? He smiled, and her stupid heart did a little skip that she firmly told it to stop doing immediately.

"Enchanted," he said, and of course his English was accented but perfect. Of course it was.

Eleanor led them through the villa, past rooms Hazel glimpsed only briefly—a library with floor-to-ceiling books, what looked like a formal dining room with a table that could seat twenty. The demonstration kitchen was at the back of the ground floor, and it took Hazel's breath away.

This wasn't just a kitchen—it was a temple to pastry. Gleaming copper pots hung from hooks. Stand mixers that looked like they could mix concrete lined one counter. Two massive ovens dominated one wall, and the central island was topped with marble perfect for rolling dough. Every surface sparkled. Every tool had its place.

"Welcome, welcome!"

The man who bustled in wore chef's whites and a tall toque that added a foot to his height. He was short and round, with rosy cheeks and hands that moved constantly as he talked. But it was his name that made everyone straighten up.

"I am Philippe Rousseau," he announced. "Yes, that Philippe Rousseau. You know my restaurants, perhaps? My books? My television program?"

Hazel didn't, but from the way Isabella actually gasped and Monique started taking photos, she was clearly the only one. Even Louis looked impressed.

"We are so fortunate," Eleanor murmured to the group, "to have Chef Rousseau as our guest chef. He's between filming seasons of his show."

"Enough, enough," Chef Rousseau waved away the attention, though he clearly enjoyed it. "We are here to make pastry, not talk about television. Though if you want signed cookbook, I have some..." He winked. "But first! We must understand each other. My English, she is not perfect. Madame Moore will help when I am—how you say—stuck for words. Yes?"

"Of course," Eleanor said.

"Bon! Now, who can tell me the most important thing in pastry?"

Hazel's hand was halfway up when Louis spoke. "Precision. Pastry is chemistry. Every measurement must be exact."

"Très bien! Very good. And what else?"

This time Hazel was ready. She opened her mouth—

"Temperature," Louis said. "Cold butter for flaky pastry, room temperature for creaming."

Hazel's jaw clenched. Okay. Fine. He wanted to be teacher's pet? She could play that game.

"And what about—" Chef Rousseau began.

"Patience," Louis interrupted smoothly. "Good pastry cannot be rushed."

Oh, come on. Hazel glared at the back of his perfectly styled head. Who did he think he was, the pastry whisperer?

"Excellent, excellent!" Chef Rousseau beamed. "I see we have some knowledge here already. This is good. Now, who knows why we sift flour?"

Hazel practically launched herself forward. "To aerate it and remove—"

"To aerate it and remove lumps," Louis finished. He had the audacity to turn and smile at her. "Also to ensure even distribution when combining with other dry ingredients."

Hazel felt her eye twitch.

"Wonderful!" Chef Rousseau clapped his hands. "Such enthusiasm! Now, let us discuss the difference between pâte brisée and pâte sucrée..."

For the next ten minutes, Louis answered every. Single. Question. Sometimes Hazel didn't even try, just watched in growing irritation as he rattled off perfect responses in his perfect accent with his perfect face.

The other students seemed to find it amusing. Isabella whispered something to Monique that made her giggle. Priya took notes with the focused intensity of someone planning corporate takeover. Xu Fei smiled serenely at everything.

"Now!" Chef Rousseau clapped again. "Enough theory. We cook! Today, we make ze classic—tarte aux pommes. Apple tart. Simple, yes? But in simple, we see skill. Choose partner, please."

The pairing happened fast. Isabella grabbed Monique immediately. Priya turned to Sofia with a resigned expression that said she'd assessed the room and made a practical choice. Yuki and Xu Fei gravitated together, already comparing notes in a mixture of English and hand gestures.

Which left...

"It seems we're partners." Louis appeared at her elbow, smiling that infuriating smile.

"Lucky me," Hazel muttered.

"Pardon?"

"Nothing." She forced her own smile. "Partners. Great. Try not to burn anything, okay?"

He studied her for a moment, that smile shifting into something more genuine. "You know, I have a feeling this is going to be more interesting than I expected."

"Interesting. Right." She turned toward their station. "That's one word for it."

6

They claimed a station at the far end of the kitchen. Hazel started gathering ingredients with the efficiency of someone who'd spent years in professional kitchens, even if hers had been less grand than this. Flour, butter, salt for the pastry. Apples, sugar, cinnamon for the filling.

"So," Louis said, measuring flour with suspicious precision for someone who supposedly knew everything, "you work in a bakery?"

"How did you—"

"I ran into Eleanor this morning. She mentioned we had an American baker joining us. From California." He glanced at her. "You're the only American here, so…"

"Ah." She watched him cube butter and noticed he was doing it wrong—pieces too big, not uniform. Interesting.

"And you came all this way to learn French pastry?" He asked.

"Seemed like a good idea at the time." She kept watching his technique. "What about you? Why are you here?"

"New Year's resolution." He kept his eyes on the butter. "I make a list every year. Learn new language, read more books, master French pastry..."

"That's quite an expensive resolution."

He shrugged, very French. "Some resolutions are worth the investment."

Hazel took over the butter, cutting it properly. "Most people just join a gym."

"I already belong to a gym." He leaned closer, lowering his voice. "Actually, can I tell you something? The resolution story is just what I tell people."

Her pulse kicked up, which was ridiculous. "Oh?"

"I'm an investor." His breath tickled her ear. "I'm considering putting money into the school. Wanted to see if it lives up to its reputation. Due diligence."

"So all that showing off earlier..."

"Research." He grinned, and it transformed his face from handsome to boyish. "I've been reading pastry textbooks for weeks. Memorizing facts. Making myself look knowledgeable."

"But you don't actually know how to bake."

"Not even a little bit."

Hazel burst out laughing. She couldn't help it. "You fraud."

"Guilty." He held up his hands in surrender. "So perhaps you could... help me? Unless you're planning to kill me. I heard you muttering something about that when I was answering questions."

"I'm considering it." But she was smiling as she showed him how to cut butter properly. "Smaller pieces. See? And keep everything cold. Use your fingertips, not your palms."

They worked the butter into the flour, and Hazel tried not to notice how his hands looked doing the work. Long fingers, surprisingly graceful. A thin scar across one knuckle.

"You're good at this," he said.

"I should be. I've been doing it since I was eight."

"Your parents taught you?"

The question hit unexpectedly. "My grandmother. My parents died when I was little."

"Ah." His hands stilled. "Mine too. Not when I was little—I was eleven. But still."

"I'm sorry."

"It was a long time ago." He resumed working the dough. "Raised by my grandparents after that. Good people, but very... traditional. They had plans for me. University, business degree, proper career."

"Let me guess—becoming an investor wasn't exciting enough?"

"Oh, they would have loved that. Very respectable." His French accent thickened with emotion. "But they're gone now too, left me more money than anyone needs. I figured I should do something with it instead of letting it sit in banks."

There was something in his voice—a kind of bitter freedom that Hazel recognized. When everyone who had expectations for you was gone, you were left with the terrifying prospect of deciding for yourself.

"I get that," she said quietly. "My grandmother just died. Three months ago. She left me... well, enough to come here. To try something new."

"To become a French pastry chef?"

31

"To become something." She pressed the dough together, forming a rough disk. "This needs to chill. Thirty minutes minimum."

They wrapped the dough and put it in one of the massive refrigerators. Around them, the other pairs were at various stages of chaos. Isabella had somehow gotten flour in her perfect hair and was laughing about it. Monique was taking photos of everything. At the next station, Priya was explaining something to Sofia with the patience of a saint.

"Oh no!"

Everyone turned. Xu Fei stood frozen, staring at her mixing bowl. Electric beaters still whirred in her hand, and what should have been pastry cream was splattered across her station, the wall, and most of Yuki's shirt.

"I think maybe—" Xu Fei said in careful English, "—too fast?"

Chef Rousseau rushed over, alternating between French exclamations and soothing English. "Is okay! Is okay! Everyone make mistake. We clean, we start again."

"I'm so sorry," Xu Fei said to Yuki, who was dabbing at her shirt with a towel.

"It's fine." Yuki actually smiled—the first time Hazel had seen her do so. "In Tokyo, I once exploded an entire batch of choux pastry. This is nothing."

That broke the tension. Everyone started sharing their kitchen disasters while they helped clean up. Monique told a story about setting a pan of sugar on fire. Isabella had once forgotten salt in bread dough and served it to her mother-in-law.

"What about you?" Louis asked Hazel as they checked their dough. "Any kitchen disasters?"

"Oh, plenty," she said, grinning at the memory of the worst one. "When I was fifteen, I tried to make croquembouche to impress my grandmother."

"Ambitious."

"Stupid. I didn't know you needed a special mold. Tried to freestyle it." She shook her head. "Caramel everywhere. And I mean everywhere. The ceiling. The dog. My grandmother's antique tablecloth."

"The dog?"

"He was trying to help. Or eat the cream puffs. Hard to tell with dogs."

Louis laughed, a rich sound that made something warm unfurl in Hazel's chest. Which was annoying. She wasn't here to develop crushes on mysterious Frenchmen with excellent bone structure. She was here to learn.

Their dough properly chilled, they rolled it out. Or rather, Hazel rolled while Louis watched with the intensity of someone memorizing technique.

"Thinner," she instructed. "And turn it as you go—like this. Keep the shape even."

"You're a good teacher."

"You're a terrible student. You're not even trying."

"I'm observing. Very different thing." But he took the rolling pin when she offered it, attempting to copy her movements. The dough immediately stuck to the counter. "Merde."

"Flour. More flour." She couldn't stop laughing. "How did you think you were going to fake your way through two weeks of this?"

"Charm?" He gave her a hopeful look. "Bribery? I brought very good wine."

"You can't bribe dough."

"Everything can be bribed. You just have to find the right currency."

They salvaged his dough, lined the tart pan, and started on the apples. This, at least, Louis could handle. His knife work was actually decent.

"University," he said when she commented on it. "Survival skill. Cook or starve."

"Oxford, right? You mentioned that earlier."

"Ah, you were listening."

"Hard not to when you were answering every single question like some kind of pastry encyclopedia."

"Jealous?"

"Annoyed."

"Same thing, really."

She threw an apple peel at him. It was childish and unprofessional and felt absolutely perfect. He caught it, grinning.

"Violence! In the kitchen! Chef, she's assaulting me with produce!"

"Focus!" Chef Rousseau called without looking up from where he was helping Isabella and Monique save their burnt tart shell. "Less talking, more cooking!"

They arranged apple slices in overlapping circles, brushed them with butter, sprinkled sugar and cinnamon. Into the oven it went. Thirty-five minutes to moment of truth.

"Now we clean," Hazel said. "First rule of professional kitchens."

"I thought the first rule was don't burn things."

"That's the second rule."

They worked side by side, washing bowls, wiping counters. The kitchen smelled like heaven—butter and cinnamon and caramelizing fruit. Through the tall windows, Hazel could see the garden, green and perfect in the afternoon sun.

"Can I ask you something?" Louis said suddenly.

"Why do I feel like you're going to anyway?"

7

"Eleanor mentioned something interesting when we spoke this morning."

"Oh?"

"She said this was your first time leaving California. First time on a plane."

"So?"

"So why here? Why now? Most Americans, they start with London. Maybe Italy. Paris is..." He gestured vaguely. "Advanced travel."

Hazel focused on drying a mixing bowl. How to explain the last three months? The grief, the discovery, the desperate need to be somewhere Bridget had never been?

"My grandmother always wanted to see Paris," she said finally. It wasn't a lie, exactly. Bridget had kept a calendar from the 1980s with Eiffel Tower pictures. "She never got the chance. So I figured…" She shrugged. "Someone should."

"That's lovely."

"That's guilt."

"Not the same thing?"

"Speaking of guilt—I think our tart might be burning."

It wasn't burning. It was perfect. Golden crust, caramelized apples arranged in a spiral that actually looked professional. Louis stared at it like it might explode.

"We made that."

"I made that. You watched."

"I was supervising. Very important job." He leaned close to examine it. "It actually looks edible."

"High praise."

"I have very low standards. You should see what I usually eat."

"Let me guess—restaurants?"

"Takeaway containers and shame." He straightened. "But this. This is art."

"This is lunch."

Around them, other teams were pulling their tarts from ovens with varying degrees of success. Priya and Sofia's looked professional. Monique and Isabella's had clearly been rescued by Chef Rousseau. Xu Fei and Yuki's was slightly lopsided but smelled amazing.

"Bon!" Chef Rousseau clapped for attention. "Now we taste! This is important—you must know what you create. How else to improve?"

They cut their tarts, arranged slices on plates. Hazel watched Louis take his first bite with the focus of a proud parent. His eyes widened.

"Oh."

"Good oh or bad oh?"

"I made this." He sounded genuinely amazed. "Well. You made this. But I helped. And it's actually good."

"Don't sound so surprised."

"But I am surprised. I don't make things. I invest in people who make things. Very different skill set."

"Maybe you're in the wrong business."

He looked at her then, really looked at her, and something passed between them. A recognition, maybe. Two orphans in a French kitchen, finding something they didn't know they were looking for.

"Maybe I am," he said quietly.

The moment stretched until Chef Rousseau's voice broke it. "Excellent work, everyone! Tomorrow, we make choux. Very technical. Very easy to fail. It will be magnificent disaster, I promise!"

Everyone laughed, the tension of the first day dissolving. They cleaned their stations—properly this time, no shortcuts. Hazel found herself working automatically, the rhythm of a professional kitchen second nature. Louis tried to help, mostly got in the way, but she didn't mind as much as she should have.

They were almost done when Charles Lambert appeared in the doorway.

He looked every inch the distinguished director—perfectly pressed shirt, silver hair gleaming in the afternoon light. His smile was warm, professional, the kind of smile that had probably charmed donors and dignitaries for years.

"How wonderful to see you all here," he said. "I trust Chef Rousseau is taking good care of you?"

"The best care," Isabella gushed. "He's amazing. This whole place is amazing."

"You're too kind." Charles moved into the kitchen. "I wanted to personally invite you all to our traditional first-night banquet. Seven o'clock in the main dining room. A chance to get to know each other better, sample some of our kitchen's specialties."

"What kind of specialties?" Monique asked. "Please tell me there's champagne."

"The best champagne," Charles assured her. "And wines from our cellar. Our chef has prepared a tasting menu that will, I hope, inspire your studies here."

His gaze swept the group and landed on Hazel. Stopped. That same flash of—something. Recognition? Confusion? Fear? It was gone before she could identify it, but she saw the way his jaw tightened, the slight tremor in his hand before he clasped them behind his back.

Charles seemed to realize he was staring and turned abruptly to address the group. "Seven o'clock, then. Don't be late. Our chef gets temperamental when his soufflé deflates."

He left quickly, and conversation resumed around Hazel. But she stood frozen, replaying those few moments. The way he'd looked at her. The tremor in his hands.

"Well," Louis said quietly beside her. "That was interesting."

"What?"

"The way he looked at you. Like seeing a ghost."

So she wasn't imagining it. "I've never met him before. I'd remember."

"Perhaps you remind him of someone."

"Maybe." But it felt like more than that. Felt specific. Personal.

"Don't look so worried." Louis touched her elbow lightly. "It's probably nothing. At our age, we all remind old people of someone. Their lost youth. Their regrets. Their—"

"Their what?"

"I was going to say their first loves, but that seems unlikely. You're far too American for his generation's taste."

"What's that supposed to mean?"

"Nothing insulting. Just that men of his age and class usually prefer their women more... how to say... contained. You have very uncontained energy."

"I can't tell if that's a compliment or not."

"Neither can I." He grinned. "Shall we go? I need to prepare for tonight. Find something suitable to wear to a banquet where the director stares at young women like they're harboring dark secrets."

"I don't have dark secrets."

"Everyone has dark secrets. That's what makes them interesting."

Hazel watched him leave, annoyed to find herself wondering what he'd wear tonight. Annoyed to find herself caring.

Seven o'clock. Banquet. Champagne and mysterious looks and probably more questions than answers.

She touched the spot on her elbow where Louis's fingers had been.

Maybe she'd find out why Charles Lambert looked at her like he knew exactly who she was.

Maybe she'd find out why that terrified him.

8

Charles left the demonstration kitchen and started up the stairs, his hand gripping the bannister tighter than necessary. The girl's face swam before him—those eyes, that particular way she'd tilted her head when laughing. His chest tightened with each step, as if the very act of climbing was squeezing the air from his lungs.

He paused at the top of the stairs, one hand pressed against the doorframe of the dining room. Fifty years old and reduced to this—catching his breath like some out-of-shape tourist who'd attempted the Eiffel Tower stairs. But it wasn't the physical exertion that had him struggling. It was the shock of recognition, the impossibility of what he'd seen.

"Monsieur Lambert? Are you well?"

The voice made him jerk upright. Madame Dubois stood just inside the dining room, polishing cloth in hand, studying him with those sharp eyes that missed nothing. The woman had an uncanny ability to materialize in rooms without warning, as if the villa itself whispered its secrets to her.

"Fine, fine." He straightened his shirt, smoothed his hair. "Just these old bones protesting the stairs."

She tilted her head, clearly unconvinced. At seventy-two, she navigated the villa's three floors with the energy of someone half her age. He'd hired her fifteen years ago, when the school was still finding its feet. She could work miracles with silver polish and knew how to manage a household with discretion, though her attentiveness sometimes bordered on the uncomfortable.

"Perhaps you should rest before tonight?" She moved closer, the lemony scent of her furniture polish filling the space between them. "The banquet requires much energy. You always give so much of yourself to the students."

"The banquet will be perfect, as always." He forced a smile. "Thanks to you."

"Naturally." She turned back to the massive oak table, running her cloth along wood that already gleamed. "The flowers will arrive at four. The Limoges china has been washed twice. I've instructed the kitchen to have the champagne at precisely the right temperature."

"I never doubted it."

She made a dismissive sound that suggested his faith was both expected and irrelevant. Charles watched her work for a moment, grateful for the distraction. The dining room looked magnificent in the afternoon light—oil paintings in gilded frames catching the sun, crystal chandelier throwing subtle rainbows across the ceiling.

"The new students," Madame Dubois said without looking up, "they seem promising. A good mix this time."

"Yes. They all seem... suitable."

"The American girl has beautiful manners. Very polite, always saying please and thank you." She moved to polish a silver candlestick. "It's refreshing. So many students now, they treat staff like furniture."

Charles's hand tightened on the doorframe. Even Madame Dubois had noticed her. Of course she had. The girl was impossible to miss.

"She seems... pleasant," he managed.

"More than pleasant. There's something about her. A quality." Madame Dubois glanced at him. "You noticed it too, I think. Last night, when she arrived. You looked as if you'd seen something unexpected."

Charles stood frozen for a moment longer, then turned and headed for the stairs. "The accounts need reviewing before tonight. Please ensure everything is ready by seven."

"Of course, monsieur."

He could feel her watching him leave, those sharp eyes cataloguing his retreat. Fifteen years she'd worked for him, and she could read him like one of her perfectly polished surfaces—every smudge, every imperfection visible.

The second floor hallway stretched before him, afternoon light filtering through tall windows. His footsteps echoed on the hardwood, each one a reminder to pull himself together. He was Charles Lambert, director of one of Europe's most prestigious pastry schools. He'd built this place from nothing, convinced investors to trust him, transformed a crumbling villa into a temple of culinary excellence. He would not let his composure crack over a resemblance, no matter how uncanny.

His office door closed with a satisfying click. Safe. He sank into his leather chair, hands flat on the desk, breathing slowly. The room smelled of leather and old books, the comforting scent of authority and achievement. Awards lined one wall—certificates, newspaper clippings, a photo of him with the President at a state dinner. Evidence of a life well-lived, a reputation carefully built.

He was being ridiculous. Paranoid. So what if the girl reminded him of someone? The world was full of resemblances, full of faces that echoed other faces. It meant nothing. It had to mean nothing.

But his hand was already reaching for the bottom drawer of his desk, the one he kept locked. The key lived on his keychain, small and unremarkable. Inside, beneath contracts and financial documents, lay a single photograph in a silver frame.

Charles lifted it out, angling it toward the window light. Four people smiled back at him, young and impossibly confident. Himself at twenty-two, still believing he could change the world one soufflé at a time. And the others...

He traced a finger over the faces, memories flooding back. The late nights in the university library, arguing about technique and innovation. The disastrous dinner party where they'd tried to flambe everything and nearly burned down the apartment. The dreams they'd shared, the promises they'd made.

All of it ended now. Gone. Except...

The resemblance was undeniable. The eyes, the bone structure, the way she held herself. Even her laugh—he'd heard it in the kitchen today—had the same musical quality. It couldn't be coincidence. The timing was right, the name, everything pointed to a connection that made his hands tremble.

But how to be certain? And if he was right, what then? What did he owe to the past?

9

Hazel held up her black dress, then tossed it back on the bed with a frustrated sigh. Too formal. She grabbed the navy blue one, held it against herself in the mirror. Too casual. The third option, a deep green wrap dress, seemed like trying too hard.

"You're being ridiculous," she told her reflection. "It's just dinner."

But it wasn't just dinner, and she knew it. This was her first real test of whether she belonged here, among these people who probably grew up attending banquets in grand estates. People who knew which fork to use without thinking about it, who could pronounce French wine names without sounding like they were choking.

She thought about this morning, the way the other students had looked in their designer clothes. Even their casual wear screamed money in that understated way that true wealth always did. Quality fabrics that draped just right, shoes that were both practical and somehow elegant. And then there was her, in her jeans and the sneakers she'd bought on sale at the outlet mall.

The inheritance sat in her bank account like a guilty secret. Technically, she could afford designer clothes now. Could walk into any boutique in Paris and buy whatever she wanted. But years of careful spending, of checking price tags and waiting for sales, didn't just evaporate because a number in her bank account had changed.

She settled on the beige dress. Simple, knee-length, the nicest thing she owned. She'd bought it two years ago for a friend's wedding, the one extravagance she'd allowed herself that year. Adding her grandmother's pearl earrings helped. Bridget had worn them every Sunday to church, and putting them on felt like carrying a piece of home with her.

Hazel applied makeup with more care than usual—a little more mascara, a touch of lipstick. Nothing dramatic. She wasn't trying to compete with Isabella or Monique. She just wanted to look like she belonged here, like she wasn't some small-town baker who'd stumbled into the wrong life.

The thought of Louis flashed through her mind, and she pushed it away. So what if he'd be there? So what if he'd probably look unfairly good in whatever he wore? She'd paid a small fortune to come here and learn from the best—not to get distracted by charming Frenchmen.

By the time she made it downstairs at exactly seven o'clock, her stomach was doing uncomfortable flips. The dining room doors stood open, voices and laughter spilling out. Hazel paused at the threshold, taking it in.

The room looked like something from a movie about rich people's problems. The chandelier she'd noticed that morning now blazed with what had to be a hundred candles. The table was set with china so delicate it looked like it might shatter if you breathed wrong. Crystal glasses caught the light, and flowers—roses and peonies and something purple she couldn't name—spilled from silver vases.

But it was the people who made her want to turn around and go back upstairs.

Isabella wore a red dress that hugged every curve. Monique had chosen silver, sleek and sophisticated. Sofia looked like she'd stepped out of a fashion magazine in cream-colored silk. Even Priya, who'd been practical in the kitchen, wore an elegant sari in deep purple.

They all looked like they belonged here. Like they'd been born knowing which fork to use and how to hold champagne flutes without looking awkward.

"Hazel!" Eleanor appeared at her elbow, gorgeous in midnight blue. "Don't you look lovely. Come, let me get you some champagne."

Before Hazel could protest that she looked like she'd gotten dressed at a department store sale rack—which wasn't far from the truth—Eleanor was guiding her into the room. The conversation continued around them, but Hazel caught a few appraising glances. Great. They were probably wondering who'd let the small-town American crash their party.

Two empty chairs remained at the table. One next to Monique, who was now holding court with a story about her ex-husband's art collection. The other beside Xu Fei, who sat quietly, looking almost as out of place as Hazel felt. Her green dress was well-made but simple, and she held her champagne glass like she wasn't quite sure what to do with it.

Hazel took the seat beside Xu Fei, grateful for the company of someone who didn't look like they'd stepped off a runway.

"Beautiful room," Xu Fei said softly. "Like dream."

"Like an expensive dream," Hazel agreed. "I keep waiting for someone to tell me I'm in the wrong place."

Xu Fei smiled. "Me too. But we are here, yes? We belong."

Hazel wanted to believe that. Wanted to feel like her tuition payment was the only credential she needed. But watching Monique laugh at something Sofia said, seeing the casual way Isabella adjusted her diamond bracelet, she felt every one of her twenty-five years in Fillmore. Every shift at the bakery, every coupon clipped, every dream deferred because there wasn't money for it.

The door opened again, and Louis walked in. Late, of course. Hazel tried not to stare and failed completely.

He wore a charcoal suit that had definitely been tailored to his exact measurements. His hair was artfully disheveled in that way that probably took twenty minutes to achieve. He moved through the room like he owned it, comfortable in his skin in a way Hazel envied.

He took the last empty seat beside Monique, who immediately shifted closer, her body language changing from casual elegance to focused interest. They looked good together—two beautiful French people who understood this world of champagne and candlelight. Monique said something in French that made him laugh, and Hazel turned her attention to her glass, annoyed at the twist in her stomach. She had no right to feel... whatever this was. Jealousy? That was ridiculous. She'd known the man for less than twelve hours.

"Welcome, everyone." Charles stood at the head of the table, champagne glass raised. He looked perfectly composed, no sign of the man who'd stared at her like she was a ghost. "To new beginnings and sweet endings. Santé!"

Everyone echoed the toast. Hazel sipped her champagne, bubbles tickling her nose. She wasn't much of a drinker, but this didn't taste like the stuff they sold at the grocery store in Fillmore.

"Now," Charles continued, "we have two weeks together. In that time, you'll learn techniques, create masterpieces, probably shed a few tears over failed soufflés." Polite laughter. "But more than that, you'll become a family. The bonds formed in kitchens are unique. So let's begin with introductions. Tell us what brought you to L'Académie."

He nodded to Isabella, who practically glowed under the attention.

"Well, I am Isabella Giuliani from Rome. My husband—he is in finance—he gave me this course for my birthday. My fortieth, but we don't mention that." She laughed, diamond earrings catching the light. "I've always loved baking, but at home, you know, we have staff. This is my chance to learn properly."

"Wonderful," Charles said. "Monique?"

"Monique Beaumont. Parisian, born and raised." She raised her glass in a mock toast to herself. "Recently divorced, fabulously single, and ready to tackle life. Why pastry school? Why not? I have time, money, and a sweet tooth. Perfect combination, non?"

The table laughed. Hazel noticed Louis watching Monique with an expression she couldn't read. Interest? Amusement? Something else?

"Sofia?"

"Sofia Andersson from Stockholm." Her accent was crisp, precise. "I've been working at the Foreign Ministry for eight years.

Diplomatic work is... intense. I decided to take a sabbatical, do something completely different. I've always baked as a hobby, heard wonderful things about this school. So here I am."

"Excellent. Yuki?"

The Japanese woman straightened. "Yuki Tanaka. I own a hotel chain in Tokyo. Small, but growing. Our guests often complain about our breakfast pastries. I decided to learn myself what we're doing wrong. Hands-on research."

"Smart approach," Charles said. "Priya?"

"Similar story, actually." Priya spoke quickly, words tumbling over each other. "Restaurant owner in London. The pastry section is our weakness. Thought I'd learn directly rather than just hire someone new."

Something about her rushed explanation felt off to Hazel. Like she'd grabbed onto Yuki's story as a convenient excuse. But maybe Hazel was being paranoid, looking for mysteries where there weren't any.

"Xu Fei?"

"I am culinary blogger from Beijing." Xu Fei's voice was soft but clear. "Many followers want to know about French pastry, French techniques. Real insider information, not just tourist perspectives. I come to learn, take pictures, share with my readers. If that is okay? I promise to be respectful."

"More than okay," Charles assured her. "We love free marketing. Just perhaps not during the actual classes—flour and cameras don't mix well."

More laughter. The atmosphere was warming, helped by the excellent champagne and the arrival of the first course—some kind of butternut squash soup that was rich and warming, with a hint of sage and brown butter.

"Louis?"

"Louis Bassett. Usually I manage... family investments." He grinned, and Hazel noticed he was looking directly at her. "But I made a New Year's resolution to learn something completely unrelated to numbers and portfolios. Pastry seemed sufficiently challenging."

"And finally, Hazel?"

Everyone turned to her. Hazel's mind went blank. The weight of their attention felt physical, all those polished people waiting for her to justify her presence here. Should she tell them about her grandmother's death? The inheritance that still felt like stolen money? The desperate need to be somewhere, anywhere, that didn't carry memories in every corner?

"I'm Hazel Chase from California. I work in a bakery—worked in a bakery." She corrected herself, remembering she'd taken indefinite leave. "My grandmother always dreamed of seeing Paris. She never got the chance, so I thought... someone should. And if I was coming anyway, why not improve my skills?"

It was mostly true. Close enough.

"How lovely," Eleanor said. "I'm sure she would be proud."

"To grandmothers," Charles raised his glass again. "And to dreams, inherited or otherwise."

The meal progressed in courses, each more elaborate than the last. Hazel found herself relaxing slightly, helped by Xu Fei's quiet companionship and the general flow of conversation around them. Isabella told outrageous stories about Roman society—who was sleeping with whom, which marriages were business arrangements, which art collections were fake. She had the gift of making gossip sound like anthropology.

Monique and Louis seemed to be conducting their own private conversation in rapid French, lots of laughter and meaningful glances. Monique kept touching his arm when she made a point, leaning close enough that her perfume probably enveloped him. Not that Hazel was watching. Not that she was counting each touch (seven so far) or noticing how Monique's laugh got lower and more intimate as the evening progressed.

"Your grandmother," Xu Fei said during a lull, "she teach you to bake?"

"Yeah. Every Sunday. It was our thing." Hazel smiled at the memory. "She was strict about it. Measurements had to be exact, techniques perfect. I used to think she was just being difficult, but now I realize she was teaching me discipline."

"Good teacher, then."

"The best."

After the main course—duck in some kind of berry sauce that made Hazel reconsider her entire understanding of flavor—people began to move around. Isabella studied the paintings with the intensity of someone who collected art. Priya and Eleanor were deep in conversation about London restaurants. Yuki stood near a large oil painting of a woman in a blue dress, champagne glass in hand, gazing at it with unfocused eyes.

Charles approached her and began explaining something about the brushwork, gesturing at the canvas, but Hazel could see Yuki's attention wandering. This was her chance. She'd been stealing glances at him all through dinner, trying to understand what had made him stare at her so strangely. Now, with everyone distracted, she could finally ask.

10

Hazel excused herself from Xu Fei and made her way across the room, weaving between abandoned chairs and careful not to knock over any of the priceless-looking objects that seemed to occupy every surface.

She waited until Yuki nodded vaguely at something Charles said and drifted away, heading for the champagne bottle with the determination of someone who'd decided tomorrow's hangover was tomorrow's problem.

"It's beautiful," Hazel said, meaning the painting.

"Yes, quite—" Charles turned, saw her, and nearly dropped his champagne. The glass tilted dangerously before he caught it, champagne sloshing. "Miss Chase. You startled me."

"Sorry. I just wanted to hear what you were telling Yuki about the painting." The lie came easily. She was getting good at those.

"Ah." He looked relieved, turning back to the portrait. "This is Madame de Pompadour. Not the famous one—her niece. Painted by a student of Fragonard, probably around 1763. See the brushwork on the dress? The way the light catches the silk?"

He talked for several minutes about technique and historical context. Hazel half-listened, gathering courage. The painting was beautiful, sure, but she hadn't crossed the room for an art history lesson. Finally, during a pause while he sipped his champagne, she said, "Can I ask you something?"

"Of course."

"Why do you look at me like that?"

The question hung between them. Charles's fingers tightened on his glass.

"Like what?"

"Like I'm someone you know. Or knew. Someone who..." She searched for words. "Someone who surprises you."

Charles sighed. "Was it that obvious?"

"Yes."

"I apologize. I've made you uncomfortable."

"Not uncomfortable. Just confused."

That was partially true. She was also curious, worried, and slightly afraid of what he might tell her. But confused covered the general feeling.

He studied her face with an intensity that should have been creepy but somehow wasn't. More like an art historian examining a painting, looking for the artist's hand in every line.

"What were your parents' names?"

The question caught her off-guard. "My parents? Why?"

"Please. It's important."

"Thomas and Olivia Chase."

Something shifted in his expression. Relief? Resignation? "I wasn't wrong, then."

"Wrong about what?"

"I knew them. Your parents. We were at university together." He took a long sip of champagne. "When I saw you last night, getting out of that car, I thought I was seeing a ghost. You look exactly like your mother. Same eyes, same way of tilting your head when you laugh. It's quite remarkable."

Hazel felt the room spin slightly. Of all the things she'd expected, this wasn't it. "You knew my parents?"

"Very well. We were close friends for several years."

"Do you know—" The words tumbled out before she could stop them. "Do you know where they got the money? They left my grandmother a fortune, transferred it just days before they died. No one knows where it came from."

Charles's expression darkened. "I don't know for certain. But I have theories."

"Theories?"

"About the money. About the accident. About why they—" He stopped, glancing around the room. "This isn't the place. Would you come to my office after the banquet? I have a photograph you should see. And we can talk properly. I imagine you have many questions."

Every atom in Hazel's body wanted to grab his arm and demand answers now. But she could see his point. The room was full of people, conversation flowing around them. This wasn't the time for family secrets and old mysteries.

"Yes. Of course. After the banquet."

"Good." He smiled, but it didn't reach his eyes. "I'll be happy to tell you what I know. Though I should warn you—you might not like all of it."

Before she could ask what that meant, he touched her shoulder gently and moved away, already calling out a greeting to someone across the room. Hazel stood alone by the painting, staring at Madame de Pompadour's smile, wondering what exactly Charles Lambert knew about her parents.

11

Back at the table, Xu Fei was photographing the dessert—some architectural marvel involving chocolate and gold leaf. "For blog," she explained. "My readers love French desserts."

"Tell me about your blog," Hazel said, desperate for distraction. Her mind kept circling back to Charles's words. Theories about the money. About the accident. What did that mean?

"Started five years ago," Xu Fei said, setting down her camera. "Just recipes at first. My grandmother's dumplings, my mother's noodles. Then I begin to travel, try new foods. Now I have maybe two million followers."

"Two million?" Hazel nearly choked on her champagne. "That's incredible."

"In China, not so much. Food bloggers very popular. Competition fierce." She smiled. "But I love it. Food is universal language, yes? Everyone understands good meal. Doesn't matter rich or poor, young or old—everyone must eat."

"That's beautiful. Do you—"

"Ladies and gentlemen!" Isabella's voice cut through the conversation. She stood by the door, slightly flushed from champagne. "The night is young, and Paris awaits! Who wants to experience the real French nightlife?"

"Define 'real,'" Eleanor said dryly.

"Clubs! Dancing! Champagne that isn't older than my grandmother!" Isabella's eyes sparkled with mischief. "Come on, we're in Paris. When in Rome—or rather, when not in Rome..."

"Count me in," Monique said immediately. "I know the perfect place. Very exclusive."

"Of course you do," Sofia laughed. "All right, I'm convinced. But only if we're back by midnight. I'm not twenty anymore."

"Midnight?" Isabella looked horrified. "The night doesn't even start until midnight!"

"I'd strongly suggest being back by one," Eleanor said with a knowing smile. "Chef Rousseau starts at nine sharp, and trust me, his voice can pierce through even the worst headache."

"Yes, mother," Isabella said, but she was grinning. "Anyone else? Hazel? You're young, you should come."

"Thanks, but I'm still pretty jet-lagged." Also, she had an appointment with Charles and a lifetime of questions. The thought of trying to make small talk in a loud club while her mind raced with possibilities made her feel exhausted.

"Louis?" Monique's voice held a note of invitation that was impossible to miss. "Surely you know all the best spots."

"Tempting," Louis said, "but I think I'll pass. Early morning jog planned."

Monique pouted prettily. "Your loss. I'm an excellent dancer."

"I have no doubt."

There was a flurry of activity as the three women gathered purses and wraps. Isabella air-kissed everyone goodbye. Monique whispered something to Louis that made him laugh. Sofia complained good-naturedly about her heels.

Then they were gone, and the room felt suddenly quiet.

"Well," Eleanor said, stifling a yawn. "I'm afraid the jet lag is catching up with me too. If you'll all excuse me?"

She left with a graceful goodnight. Yuki stood next, swaying slightly. The champagne had clearly won its battle with her equilibrium.

"I think perhaps too much champagne," she said carefully. "Room is spinning little bit."

"Let me help you upstairs," Louis offered, already standing. "Can't have you falling on those stairs."

"Very kind."

They left together, Yuki leaning on Louis's arm. Hazel watched them go, trying not to notice how gentle he was with her, how he matched his pace to her unsteady steps. She turned back to find Xu Fei watching her with a knowing expression.

"He seems nice," Xu Fei said mildly.

"Who?"

"You know who."

Hazel felt heat rise in her cheeks. "I don't know what you mean."

"Okay." Xu Fei's smile suggested she wasn't fooled. "If you say so."

At the head of the table, Charles and Priya were engaged in what looked like an intense discussion. Their voices were low, but Priya's body language screamed frustration. She kept gesturing sharply, and Charles's responses, whatever they were, only seemed to agitate her more.

Suddenly Priya stood, chair scraping against the floor. "Fine. If you won't even consider it, then we have nothing more to discuss," she said, loud enough for them to hear. "Such a waste of—"

She cut herself off, apparently remembering they had an audience. Without another word, she strode from the room, anger in every line of her body.

Charles rose more slowly. "I should…" He gestured vaguely after Priya. "Can't have students upset on the first night. Please, enjoy the evening."

He left too, and then it was just Hazel and Xu Fei in the candlelit room.

"Interesting first day," Xu Fei observed.

"That's one word for it."

They chatted about safer topics—favorite desserts (Xu Fei loved French macarons, Hazel was partial to a good chocolate cake), travel plans, the differences between Chinese and American portion sizes.

Louis returned, reporting that Yuki was safely in her room, "Sleeping like baby. Or like woman who had entire bottle of champagne."

"She'll regret that tomorrow," Hazel said.

"Chef Rousseau will make sure of it." Louis dropped into the chair Monique had vacated. "So, ladies. How do we spend our evening? Cards? Gossip? Plot someone's murder?"

"That's not funny," Hazel said automatically.

"Everything's funny if you're French enough." He grinned at her. "You should have gone with them. Monique knows all the best places."

"I'm sure she does."

"Jealous?"

"Of Monique? Please. I just—" She stood abruptly, suddenly exhausted by the evening's emotions. "I think I'll head up to bed. The jet lag is really hitting me."

"Already? The night is still young," Louis said, but his tone was teasing rather than insistent.

Hazel ignored the knowing look in his eyes. "Xu Fei, it was nice talking with you."

"Same. Sleep well?"

"You too."

Hazel left the dining room, pulse quickening. But instead of heading to her room, she found herself thinking about Charles's invitation. He'd said to come to his office after the banquet. Should she wait longer, or was now late enough? He'd gone after Priya, but surely he'd be back by now?

The villa felt different at night. Shadows pooled in corners, and her footsteps echoed on the marble stairs despite her careful tread. She reached the second floor and hesitated at the top of the stairs. The hallway stretched before her, most doors closed and dark. But there—right near the staircase, light spilled from under a door that stood slightly ajar. The warm glow drew her forward. As she got closer, she could see a brass nameplate: *Director*. Charles's office.

He must have gone back there after talking to Priya. This was her chance to finally get some answers about her parents. She approached the door, gathering her courage.

She knocked softly. "Mr. Lambert? It's Hazel. You said we could talk after the banquet?"

No answer.

"Mr. Lambert?"

She pushed the door open, took one step inside, and screamed.

Charles sat behind his desk, eyes open but unseeing. A knife handle protruded from his chest, and blood—so much blood—soaked through his white shirt.

Hazel's scream echoed through the villa, sharp and terrible in the quiet night.

12

Louis Bassett had been trying to decide if Xu Fei's stories about Beijing street food were actually interesting or if he was just that bored when the scream shattered the comfortable quiet of the dining room.

Xu Fei's teacup clattered against its saucer. "What was that?"

"Sounds like it's coming from upstairs." Louis stood. The scream continued—high, desperate, the kind of sound that made your spine straighten whether you wanted it to or not.

"That sounds like Hazel." Xu Fei was already moving toward the door. "We should check what's happening."

They took the stairs two at a time. The screaming grew louder, more ragged, leading them to the second-floor hallway like a terrible beacon.

The director's office door stood open. Hazel was just inside, hands pressed to her mouth, whole body shaking. Her screams had dissolved into gasping sobs.

"Oh my God." Xu Fei stopped so abruptly Louis nearly crashed into her. "Oh my God, is that—"

Charles Lambert sat behind his desk, but something was wrong with the picture. His white shirt had bloomed red, and a handle—ornate, silver—protruded from his chest. His eyes stared at nothing.

Xu Fei made a sound somewhere between a gasp and a moan, her hand flying to her throat. "He's... he's dead. Oh God, he's actually dead."

Louis moved past her to Hazel, who was still making those awful sounds. He wrapped his arms around her, pulling her away from the doorway. "Hey. Hey, it's okay. Don't look. Come on, don't look at him."

Hazel buried her face in his shoulder, her whole body trembling. He could feel her trying to get control, fighting for each breath. Her fingers clutched at his jacket like she was drowning. After what felt like hours but was probably only seconds, the sobs quieted to shaky breathing.

"Xu Fei." Louis kept his voice steady. "Can you hold her for a minute? I need to call the police."

Xu Fei nodded, face pale but determined. She took Hazel's arm, guiding her further from the office door. "Come, sit down. Here, on the floor is fine. Just breathe."

Louis pulled out his phone, fingers surprisingly steady as he dialed. The French emergency number connected immediately.

"Police? Yes, we need—there's been a death. A murder. Villa Montmorency. The Academy. L'Académie de la Pâtisserie

Française." His French felt rusty, formal. "Charles Lambert. The director. He's been stabbed."

Footsteps in the hallway. Eleanor appeared in a silk dressing gown, hair in disarray. "What on earth is all this noise? It's past mid—"

"Charles est mort," Louis said, switching to French. "Someone killed him."

The color drained from Eleanor's face. "No. No, that's not—Charles?" She pushed past him toward the office. Louis caught her arm.

"Don't. You don't want to see."

"Let me go! I need to—Charles!" Eleanor's voice cracked. "Oh God, Charles, no. No, no, no." She sagged against the doorframe, tears streaming down her face. "This can't be happening. Not Charles. Not like this."

Louis found himself in the middle of chaos. Eleanor was sobbing now, harsh and uncontrolled.

"The police are coming," Louis said, in English for Hazel's benefit. "We need to stay calm."

"Calm?" Eleanor's laugh was bitter. "Charles is dead and you want me to be calm?"

Xu Fei looked between them all, still pale but holding it together better than the others. "Should we... should we wake the others?"

"The police will handle that." Louis ended the call. His jacket was damp where Hazel had cried against it.

They waited in a strange tableau: Eleanor weeping against the wall, Xu Fei sitting on the floor with Hazel, Louis standing awkwardly between them all. Somewhere a clock chimed—half past eleven? Midnight? Time had gone strange. Through the tall windows, Paris glittered on, oblivious to the horror in this room.

The police arrived in a wave of blue uniforms and rapid French. The first officers secured the scene, stringing tape across the office door, taking photos, speaking into radios. More arrived—crime scene techs in white coveralls, a photographer, people with cases of equipment Louis couldn't identify. The villa transformed from an elegant school to a crime scene.

A uniformed officer approached them. "Who discovered the body?"

"I did." Hazel's voice was small but steady. "I came to talk to Mr. Lambert and found him…"

"We'll need to speak with everyone in the building." The sergeant's English was accented but clear. "Is there somewhere we can conduct interviews?"

Eleanor pulled herself together with visible effort. "The dining room. Or the entrance hall—it's larger."

"The entrance hall. Please gather everyone there."

It became a process of waking and explaining. Yuki answered her door after several knocks, blinking owlishly. "What? What's happening? Why are police here?"

Priya's face went tight when she heard the news. "Charles is dead? But I just—when? How?"

The kitchen staff had to be summoned—Chef Bernard and his two assistants who'd prepared the banquet. They stood in a worried cluster, whispering in French. Madame Dubois appeared in a black dress, as if she'd anticipated mourning. Her face showed no surprise, only a grim sadness.

The entrance hall became an impromptu waiting room. Officers took over the space, setting up a folding table, organizing paperwork. The chandelier that had seemed magical this morning now cast harsh shadows. One by one, they called people forward for questioning.

Louis found himself across from a young officer with a notebook. The questions were straightforward—name, nationality, purpose of visit.

"I'm here for the pastry course. Two-week intensive." Louis kept his answers simple, factual.

"How long have you known Monsieur Lambert?"

"I met him yesterday. Well, the day before yesterday now. When I arrived for the course."

"And this evening? Can you describe your movements?"

"We had a banquet. Started at seven. I stayed until..." Louis thought back. "Maybe ten-thirty? Yuki Tanaka had too much champagne. I helped her to her room—she's on the third floor. Room twelve, I think. Then I went back to the dining room."

"Who was still there?"

"Xu Fei. Hazel Chase had been there too but left shortly after. Xu Fei and I talked for a while. Then we heard screaming from upstairs."

"What time was this?"

"I'm not sure exactly. Eleven? We ran upstairs and found Hazel in Monsieur Lambert's office. She'd discovered the body."

"Did you enter the office?"

"Only a step or two. To see what had happened. Then I called the police."

More questions followed—had he seen anyone near the office, heard any unusual sounds, noticed anything missing. Louis shook his head to all of them.

The entrance hall felt smaller with so many people crammed into it. The kitchen staff huddled together, shooting nervous glances at the police. Madame Dubois sat perfectly straight, answering questions with the same precision she probably brought to silver polishing. Priya kept touching her ear, then catching herself and lowering her hand.

Time crawled. The officer finished with him, moved on to Xu Fei. Louis stayed in his chair, unsure if he was allowed to move. The whole thing felt surreal.

He found himself watching Hazel across the room. She was still being interviewed, another officer questioning her while Eleanor translated. Even from across the room, Louis could see the tremor in her hands as she accepted a glass of water that Xu Fei had brought her.

Poor girl. First time abroad and she walks into something like this.

He should probably talk to her later. Make sure she was all right. It was basic human decency. Besides, she seemed nice enough, if a bit overwhelmed by everything. First time in Paris—she deserved better than this. Maybe he could show her around tomorrow. A café, some tourist spots. Remind her that the city was more than crime scenes and police interviews.

Yes. That's what he'd do. It was the decent thing to do.

13

Hazel answered the officer's questions like she was reading from a script. Yes, she'd found the body. No, she hadn't touched anything. Yes, she'd screamed. The words came out flat, automatic, while her mind churned through what had happened.

Charles was dead. Actually dead. Murdered. She'd talked to him just hours ago, and now he was gone, taking all his secrets with him. All those promises about her parents, about theories and old photographs—gone forever, silenced by a knife to the chest.

The finality of it hit her like a physical blow. For three months—ever since she'd learned about the money—she'd had so many questions. Who her parents really were, where the fortune came from, why they'd died so young. And then Charles—Charles had known them. Had answers. Had been willing to share them.

Now those answers were as dead as he was.

She thought about fate, how cruel it was. To finally find someone who knew the truth, only to have him murdered hours later. Was she cursed? First her parents, then her grandmother, now the one person who could have told her the truth about her family. Death seemed to follow her, stealing everyone who might have given her answers.

Her hands shook as she accepted the glass of water Xu Fei offered. The cool liquid helped ground her, pull her back from the edge of something that felt dangerously close to hysteria.

She couldn't stop seeing it. The knife—no, not a knife. It had been too ornate, too deliberate. A dagger. She'd noticed the empty stand on his desk, the kind of thing that might hold a letter opener or decorative blade. A gift, probably. Which meant the killer hadn't come prepared. They'd used what was at hand. Grabbed it in a moment of rage, perhaps. Or calculation. Either way, Charles was just as dead.

Her grandmother's death rose up in her memory. Finding Bridget that morning, how still she'd been. But that was different. Natural. Peaceful, even, if death could be such a thing. Bridget had been eighty-two, tired, ready. They'd had time to say goodbye, in their way. All those years together, all those Sunday baking sessions. At least Hazel had those memories.

With Charles, she had nothing. A few hours of recognition, a promise of revelation, then blood and silence.

This wasn't peaceful. This was violence. Intent. Someone had wanted Charles dead badly enough to pick up that dagger and drive it into his chest.

A nervous laugh bubbled up. She pictured one of the neighbors, some Saudi prince in his pajamas, sneaking through the garden to murder the pastry school director. The officer interviewing her raised an eyebrow.

"Sorry. I just—sorry."

Eleanor murmured a translation. The officer nodded and continued his questions. Where had she been, who had she talked to, when had she last seen Charles alive?

Hazel let her gaze wander the room as she answered. Someone here had done this. Had to be. She'd seen how strict the security was at the villa's entrance. This wasn't a random break-in.

Who, then?

Not Xu Fei. They'd been together since the others left. Isabella, Monique, and Sofia had gone clubbing—they had an alibi. Unless they'd somehow snuck back? But that seemed needlessly complicated.

Eleanor had claimed jet lag, gone to her room. Convenient. She'd known Charles for fifteen years. That was a long time to build up resentments, secrets, reasons to want someone dead. All those tears could be guilt as much as grief.

Yuki had been drunk. Or had she? Louis had helped her upstairs, but what if it was an act? What if they'd planned it together? No, that didn't make sense. They'd only just met.

Unless they hadn't just met. Unless—

Stop it. She was seeing conspiracies everywhere.

The kitchen staff seemed unlikely. They'd been cleaning up, probably eager to go home. Why would they kill their employer?

Madame Dubois even more so—the woman had to be seventy, and she'd seemed genuinely fond of Charles when she'd served lunch after their morning class. Hazel remembered how the housekeeper had smiled when speaking about "Monsieur Lambert" and his particular way of wanting the bread sliced.

Which left Priya.

Hazel watched the woman from the corner of her eye. Priya sat stiffly, hands folded in her lap. Every so often, she touched her ear—a nervous tic? Her dark hair was still perfectly styled despite the late hour, but there was something brittle about her composure. Like she was holding herself together through sheer will.

She'd argued with Charles at the end of the banquet. Left angry. Charles had followed. And then what? Had they continued their argument in his office? Had it escalated? Hazel tried to remember exactly what she'd heard. Something about waste, about Charles not considering something. A business proposal? A complaint about the school?

The pieces fit too neatly. Priya had opportunity—she was one of the last to see Charles alive. She had some kind of motive, even if Hazel didn't understand it yet. And now she sat there, touching her ear repeatedly, like something was missing.

Like she'd lost something in Charles's office.

Like she'd lost something in a struggle.

The thought made Hazel's stomach turn. Could she be sitting mere feet away from a murderer? Was Priya calculating her next move, wondering if anyone had noticed her nervousness? Or was she innocent, traumatized like the rest of them, and Hazel was creating a killer out of coincidence and anxiety?

Real life was messy, complicated. But sometimes the obvious answer was obvious for a reason. Sometimes the person who looked guilty actually was guilty.

Priya touched her ear again, caught herself, clasped her hands tighter.

Yes, Hazel thought. Something was definitely missing. And Priya knew it.

14

The detective arrived like weather—sudden and impossible to ignore. He had to be pushing seventy, with a face that had seen too much and white hair that looked like he cut it himself. His suit was rumpled but clean, and he moved with the careful dignity of someone whose knees had opinions about stairs.

He spoke to one of the officers in French. The officer gestured toward Hazel. Of course. Find body, become prime suspect. Classic.

The detective approached with measured steps. Eleanor said something to him in rapid French.

"Madame Moore." His English was accented but precise. "I appreciate your concern, but after forty years with the police, I believe I can manage an interview without translation."

"Of course, Detective—"

"Arnaud. Detective Inspector Arnaud. And frankly, I did not expect to investigate a murder in the Villa Montmorency. One month before retirement. The universe has a sense of humor."

Eleanor retreated. Detective Arnaud pulled up a chair across from Hazel. Up close, she could see the weight of those forty years in the lines around his eyes. This was a man who'd seen everything, who'd probably heard every lie a suspect could tell.

"Mademoiselle Chase. Hazel Elizabeth Chase, according to my officer. From California. First time in Paris."

"Yes."

"An eventful first visit."

"Not exactly what I had in mind."

"I imagine not." He studied her with pale blue eyes that missed nothing. "Tell me about finding the body."

Hazel went through it again. The banquet ending, people scattering, her search for Charles. The door ajar. The blood. Her voice stayed steady, but she could feel her hands trembling in her lap.

"Why were you looking for Monsieur Lambert?"

Careful. "He said he knew my parents. They died when I was young. He offered to tell me about them."

"At this hour of the night?"

"He said after the banquet. I thought—I was eager to hear what he knew."

"These parents who died when you were young. How?"

"Car accident. When I was two."

"And Monsieur Lambert knew them how?"

"University, he said. They were friends."

Arnaud made a note in a small leather notebook. "You arrived when?"

"Night before last."

"And this was your second encounter with Monsieur Lambert?"

"Yes. We met briefly when I arrived, then at the banquet tonight."

"Yet he offered to share personal information about your deceased parents after knowing you for less than twenty-four hours."

The way he said it made it sound suspicious. Hazel felt heat rise in her face. "He recognized me. Said I looked like my mother. Exactly like her, actually."

"Ah. And you believed him?"

"Why wouldn't I?"

"No reason. Tell me about the banquet. Who left when?"

Hazel walked through it. Isabella, Monique, and Sofia leaving for the clubs. Eleanor claiming jet lag. Louis helping Yuki upstairs. Each departure suddenly seemed suspicious under the detective's steady gaze.

"And Madame Patel? The one who argued with Monsieur Lambert?"

"She left angry. He followed her."

"You saw this?"

"Yes. Xu Fei and I were the only ones still at the table."

"What was the argument about?"

"I don't know. They were speaking quietly. But she was clearly upset."

"And then?"

"I stayed in the dining room with Xu Fei. We talked. Louis came back. I decided to look for Charles."

"Why then? Why not wait until morning?"

"I was anxious to hear what he knew. He was going to show me a photograph. He seemed... urgent about it."

"So anxious you couldn't wait for daylight."

"Is that a crime?"

"Not at all. Just interesting." Arnaud leaned back. "You work in a bakery."

The change of topic threw her. "Yes. I mean, I did. I'm on leave."

"For how long?"

"I haven't decided."

"Open-ended leave. How nice. Your employer must be very understanding."

"It's a small bakery. Family-run. They said to take the time I need."

"After your grandmother's death."

How did he know that? "Yes."

"My condolences. She raised you?"

"Yes."

"And left you an inheritance. Enough to afford a course that costs—what? Fifteen thousand euros?"

"Something like that." Hazel felt like she was being cross-examined in court. Every answer seemed to make her look more suspicious.

"A generous inheritance."

"My grandmother was careful with money."

"Indeed. And your parents? What did they do?"

"I don't know exactly. I was two when they died."

"Your grandmother never spoke of them?"

"Not much."

"How curious. Most grandparents love to share stories."

Hazel felt like she was being herded toward some trap. "She found it painful. Talking about her dead son."

"Understandable. And now you're here, in Paris, taking a pastry course, and the one person who claimed to know your parents ends up dead. The very night he promises to tell you about them."

"I didn't kill him."

"I didn't say you did." Arnaud smiled, but it didn't reach his eyes. "Tell me, Mademoiselle Chase. Do you make a habit of discovering bodies?"

"What? No!"

"Just checking. You'd be surprised how often history repeats itself. Some people are magnets for death. Through no fault of their own, of course."

An officer approached, holding something in an evidence bag. Arnaud took it, examined the contents through the plastic. Even from her angle, Hazel could see it was jewelry. "Mademoiselle Chase, is this yours?"

An earring. Pearl drop, elegant. "No."

"You're certain?"

Hazel touched her ears. "I'm wearing both of mine. See?"

Arnaud nodded slowly. He was about to speak when Priya stood abruptly.

"That's mine." Her voice was strained. "That's my earring."

Everyone turned to look. Priya's hand went to her left ear, where indeed only one pearl drop hung.

Arnaud's attention shifted like a searchlight finding a new target.

15

The detective moved to Priya with the measured steps of someone who'd learned not to spook suspects. He spoke quietly, gesturing for her to follow him to a corner of the entrance hall. Hazel would have given anything to hear that conversation.

Priya's earring in Charles's office. If she'd lost it during their argument, that placed her at the scene. If she'd lost it after...

But then, wouldn't she have taken it with her? Why leave evidence behind? Unless she hadn't noticed it falling. Unless the murder was unplanned, impulsive. Grab the dagger, strike, flee before thinking about what you might have dropped.

Hazel's head was starting to pound. Too much champagne at dinner, too much adrenaline after. Her nice beige dress felt wrinkled and wrong, like she was wearing a costume that no longer fit the scene. The entrance hall, so grand this morning, now felt like a trap. All of them caught here together, suspects and victim alike.

She watched Detective Arnaud question Priya, noting the woman's rigid posture, the way she kept her hands clasped to stop them from shaking. Whatever she was saying, it was taking effort. The detective nodded occasionally, made notes, his expression giving nothing away.

The front door opened. Chaos in designer heels.

"Oh my God!" Isabella's voice, pitched high with alcohol and shock. "What are the police doing here? Has someone been robbed?"

Monique and Sofia followed, equally unsteady. One of the officers moved to intercept them. Isabella's lipstick was smudged, and Monique had lost one of her shoes somewhere. They looked like what they were—three women returning from a night of clubbing, completely unprepared for what awaited them.

"There's been an incident," the officer said in careful English. "Please come in."

"Incident?" Sofia's voice was sharp despite the alcohol. "What kind of incident?"

Eleanor stepped forward. "Charles is dead. Someone killed him."

The silence lasted three seconds. Then Monique screamed. Not the controlled gasp of someone performing shock, but a raw, gulping sound. "No! Charles? Our director?"

"I'm afraid so." Eleanor's own composure was fraying. "The police need to speak with everyone."

"But we just saw him!" Isabella's face had gone pale under her perfect makeup. "At the banquet! He was right there, pouring champagne, telling stories!"

"When?" Sofia demanded. "When did this happen?"

Eleanor answered, her voice hollow. "About two hours ago. Maybe less."

"While we were—" Monique pressed a hand to her mouth. "Oh God. We were dancing while Charles was—We were laughing and drinking and—"

She didn't finish. Didn't need to. The guilt of the living, celebrating while someone died.

The officers separated them, began the questioning process again. Hazel watched Monique try to answer questions while tears carved tracks through her foundation. Watched Isabella gesture wildly, her musical Italian accent thick with distress. Watched Sofia stand rigid, answering in clipped sentences like a diplomat giving a press conference.

They hadn't done it. Couldn't have. They'd been gone, out in the city with dozens of witnesses. Unless—

Stop. She had to stop seeing murder plots everywhere. This wasn't a game. Charles was really dead, and someone in this room had really killed him. She didn't need to invent elaborate conspiracies when the simple answer was probably the right one.

Detective Arnaud finished with Priya and moved on to the kitchen staff. Priya returned to her chair, movements careful, controlled. She didn't look at anyone. Her hand went to her ear again, then dropped. A guilty gesture? Or just nervous habit?

Finally, when the last interview concluded, Arnaud stood in the center of the room, looking tired. Even master detectives, apparently, felt their age at two in the morning.

"The crime scene team will work through the night," he said. "Tomorrow, we'll have more questions. For now, you're free to return to your rooms. I strongly advise that no one leave the villa—we'll need to conduct follow-up interviews, and it would be…

inconvenient if we had to track people down across Paris. Understood?"

Murmurs of agreement. Eleanor stepped forward.

"Everyone. I know this is—" She stopped, swallowed hard. "This is a nightmare. Charles was my friend. My mentor. I can't believe—"

Another pause. When she continued, her voice was steadier. "According to the school's bylaws, I'm now acting director. I need to make decisions about the course, but I can't think straight. Not tonight."

"We should cancel," Priya said quietly. "Out of respect."

"We flew here for this," Isabella protested, wiping at her ruined mascara. "I mean, not that Charles isn't—wasn't—but we paid. The nonrefundable deposit alone was—my husband will be furious if I come home early."

"Isabella!" Monique hissed.

"What? I'm being practical. The refund process will be a nightmare. International transfers, bank fees—and some of us rearranged our lives for this. I told my children Mommy was going to learn to make proper French pastries. What do I tell them now?"

"A man is dead!" Sofia's voice cracked with exhaustion and strain. "Our teacher is dead!"

"Charles wasn't our teacher," Xu Fei said softly. "He was the director. Chef Rousseau is our teacher. The course could continue without Charles, if we wanted. From a practical standpoint."

Everyone looked at her. She flushed but continued. "I'm only saying, the course could continue. If people wanted. I flew twelve hours from Beijing. My visa is only for a month. It would be... complicated to change everything now."

"That's ghoulish," Priya said.

"It's practical," Monique countered. "I already arranged childcare for two weeks. My ex-husband is watching our son—do you know what I had to promise him to make that happen? Going home now would be a nightmare."

"Complicated for all of us," Louis agreed. "I cleared my calendar. Made arrangements."

Eleanor held up a hand. "Let's vote. Anyone who wants to leave will receive a full refund, I promise. Charles would insist on that. But if some want to stay, we could continue. Finish what Charles started. He loved this school. He wouldn't want—"

She cut herself off. Started again. "Those in favor of continuing?"

Isabella's hand shot up immediately. Then Monique's. Sofia sighed and raised hers. "I suppose I'm already here. And Charles would want the school to continue."

Xu Fei nodded. Louis, after a moment, lifted his hand. "It seems wrong to let his death end everything he built."

"Yuki?" Eleanor asked gently.

Yuki blinked slowly. She'd sobered somewhat but still looked dazed. "I don't care. Whatever everyone decides. I need to sleep."

That was five and a half for continuing. Priya sat frozen.

"I—" She touched her ear again, the one missing its earring. "I suppose. If everyone else wants to stay. It would look strange if I was the only one to leave, wouldn't it?"

Six and a half.

Everyone looked at Hazel. She could feel the weight of their attention, their exhaustion, their need for this to be over. Part of her wanted to flee. Get on the next plane home, forget this nightmare, go back to her safe small life in Fillmore.

But Charles had known her parents. Someone in this room had killed him before he could tell her why they'd died, where the money had come from, what secrets they'd been hiding. She thought of the urgency in his voice when he'd promised to show her that photograph. The way he'd said she might not like what he had to tell her.

Now she'd never know. Unless...

Unless she found out who killed him. Unless she stayed and watched and listened and learned. Not just pastry techniques, but the truth about Charles Lambert's death. And maybe, just maybe, the truth about her parents too.

"I'll stay," she said.

Because someone had murdered Charles Lambert. Someone had stolen her chance to learn about her parents. Someone thought they'd gotten away with it.

Hazel was going to prove them wrong.

16

Priya Patel sat on the edge of her perfectly made bed, hands pressed against her temples. The room spun slightly—not from alcohol, she never drank much—but from the weight of what had happened. What might have happened. What she couldn't remember happening.

She should pack. Right now. Throw everything into her suitcase and get the first Eurostar back to London. She had the perfect excuse—a murder at the school. Who would suspect her of running away from genuine danger?

Everyone. That's who.

The detective's pale eyes had bored into her when she'd claimed her earring. She'd seen the calculation there, the immediate suspicion. Running now would be as good as signing a confession.

Her phone sat on the nightstand, screen dark. She could call James, her manager. Tell him to handle things for another two weeks. He was competent enough, even if he did have an irritating habit of rearranging her carefully planned menus. Or she could call her therapist. Dr. Pearson would take an emergency session, especially if Priya explained about the blank space.

The blank space. God.

She'd been so careful. Years of therapy, breathing exercises, meditation apps. She'd learned her triggers, developed coping mechanisms. The anger was still there—it always would be—but she'd built walls around it. Containment. Control.

Until last night.

Priya stood and walked to the window. The garden below looked like something from a magazine, all manicured hedges and gravel paths. Nothing like the wild tangle of her grandmother's garden in Delhi, where she'd spent summers before her parents decided India wasn't refined enough for their daughter. Before they'd shipped her off to Bramley Hall at age eleven.

Bramley. Even thinking the name made her jaw clench.

She'd expected better from a school that charged forty thousand pounds a year. Surely children of diplomats and CEOs and minor royalty would have some sophistication. Some basic human decency.

Instead, she'd found Rachel Wheeler and Annie Walsh. Blond, vicious, and clever enough to keep their cruelty subtle when teachers were watching.

"What's that smell?" Rachel would wrinkle her perfect nose whenever Priya walked past. "Oh, it's just the curry girl."

"My mother says they have different hygiene standards," Annie would stage-whisper during swimming lessons. "It's not their fault, really."

Small things. Death by a thousand cuts. The teachers saw nothing, or chose to see nothing. Priya's parents, thrilled their daughter was mixing with the "right sort," dismissed her complaints. "Don't be so sensitive, darling. You need to learn to fit in."

She'd tried. God, how she'd tried. Stopped bringing her grandmother's samosas for lunch. Begged her mother to buy the same clothes the other girls wore. Straightened her hair until it broke. None of it mattered. To them, she'd always be different. Less than.

The first blank space had happened in the second-floor bathroom. She'd been washing her hands when Rachel and Annie cornered her.

"We need to talk about the smell in our dorm room," Rachel had said, blocking the door.

"I don't smell," Priya had replied, voice steady despite her racing heart.

"That's what you think." Annie had smiled, showing perfect teeth. "But we've all noticed. Even Matron said something."

A lie. Matron hadn't said anything. But the words hit their target anyway.

"Maybe if you showered properly—" Rachel had started.

That's where the memory cut off. One moment Priya was standing at the sink, rage building like pressure in a kettle. The next, she was being pulled off Annie by a horrified teacher. Both girls were on the floor. Rachel's nose was bleeding. Annie had scratch marks down her cheek.

"She went mental!" Rachel had sobbed. "We were just talking and she attacked us!"

Three weeks suspension. A note in her permanent record. Her parents' disappointment sharp as glass. "This isn't how we behave, Priya. This isn't who we raised you to be."

But it happened again. And again. Always when the rage hit that particular pitch. Always when someone pushed just the right buttons. She'd defended Amara from Nigeria when the boys made monkey noises. Blank space. She'd confronted the group of girls who kept "mispronouncing" Xiao Mei's name. Blank space.

By university, she'd learned to manage it better. Therapy helped. Meditation helped. Building a successful restaurant, proving all those Bramley snobs wrong—that helped most of all.

She'd been clean for five years. No episodes. No blank spaces. Just normal anger that she could feel and process and control.

Until Charles Lambert had smiled that condescending smile and said, "I'm afraid that's impossible, my dear."

His tone—polite, dismissive, final. As if she'd asked for something outrageous instead of making a perfectly reasonable business proposal. As if the obscene amount of money she'd paid for this course didn't entitle her to at least a conversation.

But Charles had refused to even consider it. Hadn't even let her finish explaining.

"The answer is no," he'd said, already turning away. "Now, shall we rejoin the party?"

The rage had hit like a physical force. That familiar pressure, that high-pitched whine in her ears. She remembered standing up, her chair scraping against the floor. Remembered fleeing the dining room. Remembered Charles catching up with her in the hallway.

"Priya, please. Let's discuss this in my office. Perhaps we can find a compromise."

She'd followed him. Of course she had—she always finished what she started. She remembered entering the office, remembered him closing the door, remembered him settling behind his desk with that patronizing smile.

And then he'd said it. "My dear, some things are more important than money. Loyalty, for instance. Honor. Concepts that perhaps are foreign in the restaurant business." That's when the whine in her ears became a roar.

And then—nothing.

The next clear memory was standing in her room, hands shaking, one earring missing. She'd touched her ear and found it gone. When? How?

Priya pressed her palms against the cool window glass. Think. Think. What happened after he'd insulted her entire profession?

But the blank space gave up nothing. Just darkness where memory should be.

The detective had the earring now. Evidence. They'd dust it for fingerprints, though hers would be expected—it was her earring, after all. The question was whether they'd found more than just the earring. She'd claimed it eagerly, too eagerly maybe, but what choice did she have? Denying it would have been worse.

She knew she'd been in that office. But what had she done during the blank space? Had she grabbed that ridiculous decorative dagger from his desk? Had she—

No. She'd never killed anyone. Not even in her worst moments, her blackest rages. Broken noses, yes. Scratches and bruises, certainly. But murder? That was a line she couldn't have crossed. Wouldn't have crossed.

Except she didn't remember. And Charles was definitely dead.

She needed to stay. Running would make her look guilty. But staying meant facing whatever was in that blank space. It meant possibly discovering she was capable of something unforgivable.

Her reflection stared back from the glass, overlaid on the perfect garden. The same face that had frightened Rachel Wheeler twenty years ago. The same hands that had done damage she couldn't remember.

What had those hands done last night?

17

Hazel woke to the sound of birds and thought for one confused moment that she was home. Then the silk sheets registered, and the canopy bed, and the fact that she'd never heard birds like these in Fillmore.

Paris. She was in Paris. And Charles Lambert was dead.

The thought hit like cold water. She'd dreamed about him all night—not nightmares exactly, but frustrating dreams where he kept trying to tell her something important but she couldn't hear over the sound of champagne glasses breaking.

Her phone showed 12:23 PM. She'd slept nearly ten hours. Her body felt heavy, like she'd been drugged, but it was probably just exhaustion and jet lag finally catching up.

She shuffled to the bathroom, avoiding her reflection. She didn't need to see what she looked like after discovering a murder victim. The shower helped, hot water washing away the lingering feel of yesterday. She'd stood in Charles's office doorway for maybe thirty seconds, but the image was burned into her retinas. The blood. The way his eyes had stared at nothing. The absolute stillness of death.

Someone knocked just as she was pulling on jeans and a Stanford t-shirt she'd bought at a thrift store. Her hands froze on the zipper. Who knocks on the door of someone who just found a body? The killer, checking if she'd seen something? The police with more questions?

Another knock, lighter this time.

"Just a second!" Her voice came out higher than intended.

She checked the peephole—a thing she'd never done before last night—and saw Louis. He stood with his hands in his pockets, looking like he'd stepped out of a casual wear catalog. Of course he looked good after witnessing a murder. Some people had all the luck.

She opened the door cautiously. "Hi."

"Good morning. Or afternoon, technically." He studied her face with those amber eyes. "How are you doing? Stupid question, I know, but I thought someone should ask."

"I'm..." What was she? Terrified? Confused? Desperate to know who'd killed the one person who could tell her about her parents? "I'm okay. Just processing."

"Processing. Very American." His smile was gentle, not mocking. "I was wondering—and please say no if this is inappropriate—but would you like to see some of Paris? Get out of here for a few hours? Eleanor gave us the day off, and sitting around here seems... unhealthy. I promise I'm an excellent tour guide."

She stared at him. Was he seriously asking her to go sightseeing? "The detective said not to leave the villa."

"Technically, he 'strongly advised' us to stay. Not quite the same as house arrest." Louis shrugged. "We'd still be in Paris. Very much in Paris, actually. Arc de Triomphe, walk along the Seine, all the tourist essentials." He tilted his head. "You can't come all this way and not see the city. Even under the circumstances."

He had a point. And the villa suddenly felt suffocating, all those rooms where Charles had walked, all those people who might have killed him. But—

"I don't think—"

The door next to hers opened and Xu Fei peered out. "Oh! Good morning. Is everything okay?"

"Louis was just asking if I wanted to see Paris," Hazel said quickly. An idea formed. Xu Fei had been with her when the murder happened. The only person she could absolutely trust. "Would you want to come? I mean, if you're not busy?"

Xu Fei's face lit up. "Really? I would love this! I need content for my blog, and my followers keep asking about Paris. When would we go?"

"Now?" Louis suggested, though Hazel noticed his smile had dimmed slightly. "If everyone's ready?"

"Let me get my camera!" Xu Fei disappeared back into her room.

The door across the hall opened and Yuki emerged, looking impossibly fresh for someone who'd been stumbling drunk just hours ago. Her hair was perfect, her simple outfit—white shirt, dark jeans—somehow elegant.

"Good morning," she said carefully. "I heard voices."

"We're going to see Paris," Xu Fei called from her room. "Would you like to come?"

Yuki blinked. "Is that... allowed?"

"We're not fleeing the country," Louis said. "Just being tourists for a few hours. It might help to get some air."

"Air," Yuki repeated. She touched her temple delicately. "Yes. Air would be good. And coffee. Lots of coffee."

"I know just the place," Louis said. "So that's four of us?"

Hazel caught something in his tone. Disappointment? Had he been hoping for something else when he knocked on her door?

"Twenty minutes?" Xu Fei suggested, emerging with two cameras around her neck. "Meet in the entrance hall?"

They agreed and scattered to prepare. Hazel closed her door and leaned against it. She was about to go sightseeing with three potential murder suspects. Well, two—Xu Fei was clear. But Yuki and Louis?

She grabbed her jacket, the one nice thing she'd bought for this trip. Navy blue, classic cut, very French according to the saleswoman at Nordstrom Rack. At the last second, she added the pepper spray from her purse to her pocket. Just in case.

Because she was going to see Paris. But she was also going to watch Louis and Yuki. See how they acted outside the villa. See if their stories from last night held up in daylight.

Someone had killed Charles before he could tell her about her parents. That someone might be about to show her the Eiffel Tower.

18

When Hazel reached the entrance hall, the others were already there. Louis was chatting with a bored-looking officer who sat by the door, scrolling through his phone. Whatever Louis said made the young man laugh and wave them through without questions.

"What did you tell him?" Hazel asked as they stepped into sunshine that felt obscenely cheerful.

"That we're going to experience true French culture by standing in line at tourist attractions and overpaying for coffee." Louis led them toward the main gate. "He said to avoid the Champs-Élysées unless we enjoy being pickpocketed."

Paris hit Hazel like a physical force. The noise first—traffic and voices and a distant siren. Then the smell—cigarettes and diesel and something baking that made her stomach growl. The street beyond the Villa's gates was narrow, lined with trees just starting to turn golden. Actual Parisian trees on an actual Parisian street.

"Okay," Xu Fei already had her camera out. "Stand there, by the wall. Natural light is perfect."

"I don't—" Hazel started.

"For my blog! My readers want to see real people in Paris, not just monuments." Xu Fei was already adjusting settings. "Louis, you too. Closer. Pretend you're friends."

"We are friends," Louis said, moving beside Hazel. "Aren't we?"

Were they? Could you be friends with someone you'd known for two days? Someone who might have committed murder?

"Sure," Hazel said. "Friends."

They posed awkwardly while Xu Fei directed them. "More natural! Talk to each other. Yuki, you stand on Hazel's other side. Perfect!"

"What do we talk about?" Hazel muttered.

"The weather," Louis suggested. "Very French. Or politics. Even more French."

"How about murder?" Yuki said dryly. "Since that seems to be the theme."

Xu Fei lowered her camera. "That's not funny."

"I wasn't trying to be funny." Yuki's expression was unreadable. "We're all thinking about it. Might as well acknowledge the elephant."

"The expression is 'elephant in the room,'" Louis said. "And yes, it's horrible. But we can't do anything about it right now. So let's see Paris and try not to let Charles's death ruin everything."

"Spoken like someone who didn't find the body," Hazel said before she could stop herself.

Louis studied her. "You're right. I'm sorry. This must be particularly awful for you."

The gentleness in his voice made her throat tight. She looked away. "Can we just go?"

"We could take the Métro or grab a taxi," Louis said after a beat. "But I'd recommend the Métro—more authentic. You haven't really seen Paris until you've survived the subway at rush hour."

"Métro sounds perfect," Yuki said. "I want the full experience."

The nearest station was a five-minute walk through streets that looked exactly like Hazel had imagined Paris would look. Narrow buildings with shuttered windows and tiny balconies. Cafés with tables spilling onto sidewalks. A woman walking three small dogs, all wearing matching bow ties. It was almost aggressively picturesque.

"First time on the Paris Métro?" Louis asked as they descended the stairs.

"First time on any metro," Hazel admitted. "We don't have subways in Fillmore. We barely have buses. Even when I visit LA, I just drive—the traffic's bad but at least I'm in control."

He showed her how to buy tickets from the machine, patiently translating the French instructions. His cologne was subtle but nice—something woody and expensive. She tried not to notice how his fingers moved confidently over the touch screen, how he automatically steadied her when someone pushed past.

The platform was crowded and stifling. Hazel pressed against the tiled wall, trying not to touch strangers. A man with an accordion was playing something mournful. Someone had left flowers on a bench—roses wrapped in newspaper.

The train arrived with a screech and a gust of hot air. Louis guided them into a car, his hand light on Hazel's back. She should probably tell him not to touch her. She didn't know him. He could be a killer. But the contact was reassuring in the press of bodies, and she was tired of being suspicious of everything.

"Five stops," he said close to her ear. The train lurched forward. "Hold the pole unless you want to end up in someone's lap."

She grabbed the metal pole just as the train took a curve. A woman with a shopping bag stumbled into her, muttering something that was probably an apology. Or a curse. Hard to tell.

"Your first metro ride and you get the full experience," Louis said. "Usually there's also someone playing violin badly or selling miniature Eiffel Towers."

"I have Eiffel Tower keychains," Xu Fei said. "From the airport. Very overpriced."

"Everything at airports here is overpriced," Yuki observed. She'd managed to find a seat and looked perfectly composed despite the chaos around her. "The coffee was ten euros. For espresso! In Tokyo, that would cause riots."

"In Tokyo, the trains run on time," Louis countered. "Here, we have character instead of punctuality."

The train stopped. People pushed off, others pushed on. A teenager with a boom box started some kind of rap performance. Hazel caught maybe one word in ten, but the energy was infectious. A few people tossed coins into his baseball cap.

"Is this normal?" she asked Louis.

"Completely. Wait until you see the ones who bring entire sound systems." He glanced at her. "You look overwhelmed."

"I'm fine." She wasn't. The noise, the smells, the constant motion—it was like being inside a living organism. "Just different from home."

"Different can be good," Xu Fei said, filming the rapper with one hand while clutching the pole with the other. "My followers love authentic city life."

They emerged from the Charles de Gaulle-Étoile metro station into chaos of a different sort. Traffic circled the Arc de Triomphe in what looked like a twelve-lane game of chicken. No lines, no apparent rules, just cars weaving between each other at terrifying speeds.

"How does anyone survive that?" Hazel breathed.

"Confidence and prayer," Louis said. "Mostly prayer. Come on, we'll take the underground passage. Much safer than playing Frogger with Parisian drivers."

The passage was lined with tourist shops selling exactly what you'd expect—berets no actual French person wore, tiny Eiffel Towers in every possible material, t-shirts with badly translated English. Hazel found herself oddly charmed by the tackiness.

They emerged at the base of the Arc. Up close, it was massive—bigger than Hazel had imagined. The carved figures seemed to writhe across the stone, all drama and patriotic fervor.

"Built by Napoleon," Xu Fei recited, already photographing. "To honor military victories."

"To honor his own ego," Louis corrected. "But it is impressive."

"Can we go up?" Yuki asked. "I'd like to see the view."

"The line's usually horrible." Louis studied the queue of tourists. "Actually, not too bad today. Maybe only a twenty-minute wait."

They joined the queue. Around them, languages mixed and merged—Spanish, German, something that might have been Polish. A group of American teenagers took selfies with the monument. A couple argued in Italian, gesturing dramatically.

"This is weird," Hazel said suddenly.

"Tourism?" Louis asked.

"Being here. Doing normal things. When Charles—" She stopped. An elderly British couple was standing very close, pretending not to eavesdrop.

"Life goes on," Yuki said quietly. "Even after death. Especially after death."

Something in her tone made Hazel look closer. Yuki's expression was distant, focused on something beyond the monument.

"Speaking from experience?" Hazel asked carefully.

"My husband died two years ago." Yuki's voice was matter-of-fact. "Heart attack at thirty-eight. Very unexpected. I thought the world would stop, but it didn't. People went to work, trains ran on time, restaurants served food. It was... instructive."

"I'm sorry," Xu Fei said softly.

"Thank you. But I'm not looking for sympathy. Just observing that tragedy doesn't stop the world. We're proof of that. Here we are, buying tickets to climb a monument while police investigate Charles's murder."

The line moved forward. Hazel studied Yuki, trying to reconcile this calm widow with the drunk from last night. Which was the real person? Or were they both real, different faces of grief?

"Is that why you drink?" The question escaped before Hazel could stop it. "Sorry. That's none of my business."

"It's fine." Yuki smiled without humor. "And yes, sometimes. Last night was... excessive. Being around happy people can be difficult. All that talk of new beginnings and following dreams. Some of us are just trying to maintain."

They reached the ticket booth. Louis paid for everyone before anyone could protest, waving away their attempts to reimburse him. "Consider it my apology for this morning. I should have realized nobody would want to be alone with a potential murderer."

"Are you?" Xu Fei asked. "A potential murderer?"

Louis grinned. "Everyone's a potential murderer. That's what makes life interesting."

19

The climb was brutal. Two hundred and eighty-four steps in a spiral so tight Hazel's shoulders brushed both walls. Her thighs burned after the first fifty. By the hundredth, she was questioning all her life choices.

"Whose idea was this?" she gasped.

"Yours, I think." Louis wasn't even breathing hard. Of course. "Or maybe Yuki's. I've lost track."

"I'm dying," Xu Fei announced from below. "Tell my followers I loved them."

"Drama queen," Yuki called from above, but she sounded winded too.

They emerged onto the observation deck like survivors of some vertical marathon. The view hit Hazel like a punch. Paris spread out in every direction, a sea of cream-colored buildings and tree-lined boulevards. The Eiffel Tower rose in the middle distance, somehow both exactly what she'd expected and completely surprising.

"Oh," she breathed.

"Worth the climb?" Louis asked.

She could only nod. The city spread before her, impossibly vast and beautiful, like someone had designed it specifically to break hearts. In the distance, the white dome of Sacré-Cœur floated above Montmartre, while the Eiffel Tower rose from the urban landscape, both landmarks defining Paris in their different ways.

"That's our neighborhood." Louis pointed northeast. "Villa Montmorency is just beyond those trees."

Strange to think of it as their neighborhood. Strange to think that somewhere in that direction, police were still processing a murder scene.

Xu Fei was in full photographer mode, switching between cameras and muttering about light angles. She conscripted them all as models again. "Lean on the railing. Look contemplative. No, not constipated—contemplative!"

"What's the difference?" Hazel asked.

"About ten thousand likes," Xu Fei said seriously.

A group of Japanese tourists asked Yuki something in Japanese. She responded, then turned to the others. "They want to know if we're famous. Apparently we look like a pop group."

"Which one am I?" Louis asked. "The brooding bad boy?"

"The one who can't dance," Yuki said. "I told them we're pastry students. They seemed disappointed."

They spent an hour on the observation deck, Xu Fei directing increasingly elaborate photos. She had them jumping in unison, pretending to hold up the Eiffel Tower, making exaggerated surprised faces. It should have been embarrassing, but something about being anonymous tourists made it fun.

"My grandmother would have loved this," Hazel said suddenly. She was leaning on the railing, watching the city move below. "She had this calendar from the 1980s with Eiffel Tower pictures. Kept it in the kitchen for decades, never threw it away. Sometimes she'd look at it while doing dishes."

"Why didn't she come?" Xu Fei asked, lowering her camera.

"Money. Time. Life." Hazel shrugged. "You know how it is. There's always next year, until there isn't."

"That's why I travel now," Yuki said quietly. "Learned that lesson. Tomorrow is a luxury, not a guarantee."

The mood had shifted. Louis seemed to sense it. "Come on. Let me show you the best view of the Tower. And there's a café that does excellent pain au chocolat. Unless anyone objects to more carbs?"

"Carbs are life," Xu Fei said firmly. "Lead the way."

The descent was easier. Hazel's legs felt like jelly, but at least gravity was on their side. They emerged into afternoon sun that had taken on a golden quality. Everything in Paris seemed to glow at this time of day.

Louis led them through streets that got progressively quieter, away from the tourist crush. The buildings here were residential, with elaborate iron balconies and window boxes full of geraniums. A cat watched them from a doorway, supremely uninterested.

"Real Paris," Louis said. "Where people actually live."

"It's so quiet," Hazel said. "I thought cities were supposed to be loud."

"Depends on the neighborhood. Rich Parisians pay for silence." He glanced at her. "Not so different from Fillmore?"

"Fillmore's quiet because nothing happens there. This is quiet because people can afford to make it that way. Big difference."

"Money makes most differences disappear," Yuki observed. "That's what my husband used to say. He was wrong about many things, but not that."

The café Louis had promised materialized on a corner, tiny and perfect. Maybe twelve tables crammed into a space that would have been a closet in America. The air inside was thick with coffee and butter.

"Quatre pains au chocolat," Louis told the woman behind the counter. "Et quatre cafés."

"Make mine a double," Yuki said. "Still recovering from last night."

They claimed the only empty table by the window. The pastries arrived warm, chocolate oozing from the layers. Hazel bit into hers and made an involuntary sound.

"Good?" Louis asked, smiling.

"These are incredible." The butter was almost obscene, rich and slightly salty. The chocolate was dark, just bitter enough to balance the richness. "And I make croissants for a living. How are these so much better than anything we do at the bakery?"

"Butter. French butter is different. Higher fat content." He took a bite of his own. "Also, these were made this morning. Probably shaped by someone who's been doing it for thirty years."

"You know a lot about pastry for someone who manages family investments," Hazel observed, putting a slight emphasis on the last two words.

He shrugged. "I pay attention. Due diligence, remember?"

"Right. Due diligence." She watched him over her coffee cup. "That's why you helped Yuki to her room last night? Due diligence?"

"That was being a gentleman." He met her gaze steadily. "She could barely walk. Someone needed to help."

"I was moving so slowly—probably took us fifteen minutes to get up to the third floor," Yuki added. "Louis was so patient, kept making sure I was steady. He even helped me get to the bed because I was swaying so badly. Made sure I was lying down safely before he left."

"See? Alibi confirmed." Louis smiled. "Why? Do you suspect me of something?"

"I suspect everyone," Hazel said honestly. "Someone killed Charles. It wasn't a ghost."

"True." He leaned back, studying her. "So who's your money on? Other than me?"

"I don't know." She shouldn't be having this conversation. But the coffee and sugar were making her bold. "Priya had opportunity. That argument seemed pretty heated."

"Arguments don't always lead to murder," Xu Fei said. "In Beijing, people argue constantly. Very few stabbings."

"But that earring," Yuki said thoughtfully. "In his office. That's damning."

"She could have lost it during the argument," Louis said. "Before the murder. Maybe someone else went to see Charles after."

"Who?" Hazel asked.

"Eleanor. She knew him best. Fifteen years of working together? That's a lot of time to build resentment." He paused. "Or Madame Dubois. She's been there forever, has keys to everything. Knows all the secrets."

"The police will check," Xu Fei said. "Camera footage, witness statements. They'll know who was where."

"Will they?" Louis challenged. "This is Villa Montmorency. Half the people living here have lawyers on speed dial. You think they'll cooperate with police trampling through their private paradise?"

He had a point. Hazel remembered the security at the gate, the general air of a place designed to keep the world out. How hard would the police really push?

"Someone saw something," she said. "Someone always does."

"Very American optimism." Louis checked his phone. "Shall we walk? The Seine is only ten minutes from here."

They paid—Louis again, despite protests—and headed back into the afternoon. The streets were busier now, Parisians heading home from work or lunch or whatever Parisians did on Friday afternoons. A woman in impossible heels rode past on a bicycle, texting one-handed.

"How does she do that?" Hazel marveled.

"Practice," Yuki said. "In Tokyo, I've seen people eat ramen while cycling. Humans adapt."

The Seine appeared suddenly between buildings, wide and gray-green in the afternoon light. Stone steps led down to a walkway along the water. Couples sat on benches, sharing wine from plastic cups. A group of teenagers had a speaker playing American hip-hop.

"This is more like it," Xu Fei said, already filming. "Real Paris life."

She started recording herself, switching between Mandarin and English. Hazel caught phrases—"beautiful city," "tragic circumstances," "my new friends." It was surreal being part of someone's content, her life repackaged for consumption by strangers in Beijing.

"Two million followers," Louis murmured. "That's impressive."

"Food blogging is competitive in China," Xu Fei said, not pausing her commentary. "You need an angle. A story. 'Chinese girl discovers French pastry' is good. 'Chinese girl solves French murder' would be better."

"That's morbid," Yuki said.

"That's business." Xu Fei lowered her camera. "Everything is content now. Even tragedy."

20

They walked along the river in comfortable silence. Or mostly comfortable. Hazel kept stealing glances at Louis and Yuki, trying to read them. Were they killers? Just fellow students? Something in between?

A boat passed, loaded with sightseers. Someone waved. Xu Fei waved back enthusiastically, then filmed it.

"For my Stories," she explained. "Engagement is important."

"Your English is really good," Hazel said. "How long have you been studying?"

"Since I was five. My parents thought it was important. 'English is the language of business. You must be fluent.'" Her impression of parental sternness was spot-on. "Jokes on them. I use it mostly to argue with people about whether Beijing duck is better than Peking duck."

"Is there a difference?" Louis asked.

"No. That's what makes the arguments so fun."

They climbed back up to street level near the Pont Alexandre III. The bridge was almost absurdly ornate, all golden statues and art nouveau lamps. More photos were required. Xu Fei directed them into increasingly ridiculous poses.

"Pretend you're in a perfume commercial," she instructed. "Very serious. Think about beautiful smells."

"I'm thinking about the metro," Hazel said. "Does that count?"

"No! Think roses. Jasmine. Fresh bread."

"Charles's cologne," Yuki said suddenly. "Did anyone else notice he wore too much? You could tell where he'd been by the smell."

The mood sobered instantly. Louis cleared his throat. "Speaking of Charles—"

"Let's not," Hazel said quickly. "Just for a few hours. Can we pretend we're normal tourists?"

"We are normal tourists," Xu Fei said firmly. "We're seeing Paris. Taking pictures. Eating pastries. Nothing abnormal about that."

"Except for the murder investigation waiting back at the villa," Yuki said.

"Which is exactly why we need this." Xu Fei adjusted her camera settings. "Mental health break. Very important. Now everyone look wistfully at the river. Yes, like that. Perfect!"

They continued along the Seine as the afternoon light turned honey-gold. Paris seemed determined to be postcard-perfect, as if the city itself was trying to distract them from last night's horror. Booksellers had set up their green boxes along the wall, selling everything from vintage posters to leather-bound classics that probably no one read anymore.

Hazel stopped at one stall, drawn by a display of old cookbooks. The covers were faded, pages yellowed with age. "Excusez-moi," she attempted in French, pointing at a book titled *Pâtisserie Traditionnelle*.

The seller, an elderly man with impressive eyebrows, launched into rapid French. Hazel caught maybe three words, none of them helpful.

"He says it's from 1962," Louis translated, appearing at her elbow. "First edition. The author was quite famous, apparently. Trained under Escoffier himself."

"How much?" Hazel asked.

More rapid French.

"Fifty euros," Louis said. "But he'll take forty because you have 'honest eyes.'"

"My eyes are honest?"

"Apparently. It's a compliment. I think."

She counted out the bills. Forty euros for a used cookbook seemed steep, even with her new inheritance. But the book was from 1962, and the seller had wrapped it in brown paper like it was precious, which maybe it was.

"Merci," she managed.

"De rien, mademoiselle." The man smiled, revealing gold teeth. "Bonne chance avec vos études."

"He wishes you luck with your studies," Louis translated as they walked away.

"How does he know I'm a student?"

"You're young, buying old French cookbooks, and look slightly overwhelmed. Easy guess."

"My French is terrible," Hazel said. "I should have studied before coming."

"Your French is charming," Louis corrected. "Very American, but charming."

"That's diplomatic for 'awful.'"

"I prefer 'authentic.'" He guided her around a jogger. "Besides, you're trying. That counts for something here."

They turned a corner and the Eiffel Tower appeared, sudden and impossible. Hazel actually gasped. She'd seen it from the Arc, of course, but up close it was different. Bigger. More industrial. More French, somehow, in its unapologetic iron boldness.

"And there she is," Louis said. "La Dame de Fer. The Iron Lady."

"It's so..." Hazel searched for words. "Structural."

"Not what you expected?"

"I expected elegant. Delicate. This is like... architectural masculinity having a feeling."

Louis laughed, that rich sound she was starting to recognize. "That's the best description I've ever heard. Mind if I steal it?"

"For what?"

"For dinner parties. My friends love talking about things they don't understand. Makes them feel cultured."

The closer they got, the more chaotic it became. Tour groups clustered around guides holding various flags and umbrellas. Vendors circled like sharks, selling miniature towers and "champagne" that was definitely not champagne. The security presence was obvious—soldiers with automatic weapons standing in groups, looking bored but watchful.

"Is that normal?" Hazel asked, nodding toward the soldiers.

"Since 2015," Louis said. "You get used to it."

A man approached them with a clipboard, speaking English with an accent Hazel couldn't place. "Excuse me, you speak English? I am student making survey about tourism. Can I ask questions?"

"Non, merci," Louis said firmly, steering them away. "Classic scam. While you're answering his 'survey,' his partner picks your pocket."

"Really?" Hazel instinctively checked her pockets.

"Welcome to Paris. Beautiful city, terrible people." He paused. "Present company excepted, of course."

They joined the moderate line for tickets. Around them, languages mixed and merged—Chinese tourists posing with selfie sticks, American families arguing about dinner plans, a group of what sounded like Ukrainians taking photos of everything.

"I need content," Xu Fei announced. "Everyone act natural while I film. Talk about something interesting."

"I once ate a whole wheel of cheese," Louis offered.

"Why?" Hazel asked, genuinely curious.

"I was twenty and someone bet me I couldn't. Turns out I could, but probably shouldn't have. Spent three days regretting my life choices."

"What kind of cheese?" This seemed important to know.

"Camembert. Good quality too. Such a waste."

"This is perfect," Xu Fei said, still filming. "Funny story about French culture. My followers will love it."

The line moved steadily. Hazel found herself relaxing, caught up in the simple pleasure of being somewhere new. The sun was warm on her face, the company was surprisingly pleasant, and for a few minutes she could almost forget why she was here. Almost forget that one of these people might be a killer.

Then she spotted them. Two uniformed police officers moving through the crowd with purpose. One of them looked familiar—the young officer who'd been taking notes in the entrance hall last night while the detective questioned everyone.

"Louis," she said quietly.

He followed her gaze. "Probably routine. This place is always crawling with police."

But the officers were heading directly toward them. The familiar one spotted Hazel and nodded to his partner. Hazel's heart rate spiked. Had something happened? Had they discovered new evidence?

The officers stopped directly in front of their group. The younger one—yes, definitely from last night—spoke first.

"You're from Villa Montmorency, yes? The pastry school? Detective Arnaud needs you back immediately."

Hazel's mouth went dry. "Why? Has something happened?"

The officer's expression didn't change. "I am not at liberty to say. But you should all return. The detective wishes to speak with everyone again."

"All of us?" Xu Fei lowered her camera.

"All students from L'Académie de la Pâtisserie Française. Immediately."

The tourists in line behind them were starting to stare. An American woman whispered something to her husband about "international incidents." Perfect. Now she was entertainment for other people's vacations.

"We'll come right away," Louis said. "Should we take the metro or—"

"A car is waiting." The officer gestured toward the street. "This way, please."

They followed in silence, their tourist afternoon officially over. Hazel's mind raced. What had the detective found? Why the urgency? And why did she have the feeling that someone's careful alibi was about to fall apart?

21

The police car crawled through the gates of Villa Montmorency at the pace of a dying snail. Louis pressed his face against the window, watching the crowd of reporters surge forward like a pack of wolves who'd caught the scent of blood.

"Jesus," he muttered. "Word travels fast in this city."

"Vultures," Xu Fei said, her cameras clutched protectively to her chest. "In Beijing, at least they pretend to have shame."

The officer behind the wheel said nothing, just gripped the steering wheel tighter as reporters pressed against the car. Their voices penetrated even through the closed windows.

"Is it true Charles Lambert was murdered?"

"Are you suspects?"

"Did you know the victim?"

"Was this a crime of passion?"

A woman with platinum blonde hair and too much lipstick actually pressed her face against Louis's window, shouting in rapid French about exclusive interviews and payment for stories. He jerked back instinctively.

"This is insane," Hazel said from beside him. Her voice was steady, but he could see her hands twisted together in her lap. "How did they even find out so fast?"

"Paris has a million eyes," Louis said. "Someone always sees, someone always talks."

The officer leaned on the horn, a long angry blast that made the reporters step back just enough for the car to inch forward. More shouting, more questions.

"Are we safe?" Yuki asked quietly. She'd been silent during the entire ride back from the Eiffel Tower, staring out the window with that distant expression she got sometimes.

"From the reporters? Probably not," Louis said, trying for levity. "They're more dangerous than any murderer."

Nobody laughed.

The car finally broke free of the crowd and pulled up to the school entrance. The villa's courtyard was mercifully empty—the security gates kept the reporters at bay. But even here, Louis could hear the distant shouts from the gate.

"Quickly, please," their driver said, speaking for the first time. "Inside."

The entrance hall looked exactly like it had last night. Officers with clipboards, students being interviewed at makeshift stations, the general air of organized chaos. But something was different. Louis spotted Detective Arnaud standing near the stairs, not interviewing anyone, just watching. Waiting.

The detective's pale eyes found Louis immediately. Not good.

"Ah," Arnaud said, approaching with those measured steps of his. "Our wandering students return. Did you enjoy your tourism?"

"We saw the Eiffel Tower," Xu Fei offered. "Very tall."

Arnaud's expression didn't change. "How delightful. And did it occur to any of you that when a police detective strongly advises you to remain at a murder scene, it might be wise to listen?"

"Your exact words were that we should stay, not that we must stay," Louis pointed out. "There's a significant legal distinction."

"Indeed." Arnaud's smile was thin as paper. "You seem very familiar with legal distinctions, Monsieur Bassett."

"I watch television."

"How educational." The detective gestured to the other officers. "We have new developments. Additional questions. We'll need to speak with each of you again."

The way he said it, the way his eyes lingered on Louis, made everything clear. They'd found something. Something that made him more than just another witness.

"Toussaint, please interview Mademoiselle Chase," Arnaud said to a younger officer. "Martin, take Mesdemoiselles Tanaka and Xu. I'll handle Monsieur Bassett personally."

Louis's stomach dropped. Personally. Just like Arnaud had personally interviewed Hazel last night after she'd found the body. Just like he'd personally interviewed Priya when her earring turned up in Charles's office.

"Something wrong?" he asked, keeping his voice light.

"Not at all. Just some clarifications needed. This way, please."

Louis followed the detective to a corner of the entrance hall that had been set up as a temporary interview space. Two chairs, a small table, nothing else. Arnaud sat with his back to the wall, gesturing for Louis to take the other chair. The position meant Louis had to sit with his back to the room, unable to see what was happening behind him. Clever.

"Let's discuss yesterday evening," Arnaud switched to French without preamble. "You helped Mademoiselle Tanaka to her room, yes?"

"Yes. She'd had too much champagne. Could barely walk."

"What time was this?"

"Around ten-thirty, maybe a bit later."

"And then?"

Louis had been through this last night, but he repeated it anyway. The slow journey to the third floor, making sure Yuki was safe, returning downstairs.

"Interesting," Arnaud said when he finished. "Because there's quite a gap between when you left with Mademoiselle Tanaka and when you returned to the dining room."

"She was very drunk. We had to stop several times on the stairs. She was swaying badly—I thought she might fall. When we finally reached her room, I helped her to the bed because she could barely stand."

"How considerate."

"Basic decency."

"And after you left her room?"

"I stopped by my room. Used the bathroom."

Arnaud's eyebrows rose slightly. "You didn't mention that in your statement last night."

"I didn't think it was relevant. I was in there for maybe two minutes."

"Every detail is relevant in a murder investigation, Monsieur Bassett. Every gap in time, every movement." The detective leaned back slightly. "Especially when we have a witness who claims to have seen someone matching your description entering Charles Lambert's office around the time of his death."

The words hit like cold water. Louis forced himself not to react, even as his mind raced. A witness? That was impossible. The hallway had been empty when he'd helped Yuki upstairs, empty when he'd returned to the dining room.

"That's not possible," he said finally. "I never went near Charles's office."

"Someone did. Someone tall, dark-haired, wearing a charcoal suit. Ring any bells?"

"Half the men in Paris fit that description."

"True. But half the men in Paris weren't in this villa last night." Arnaud pulled out his notebook, flipped through pages. "Were you aware that Monsieur Lambert often worked late in his office?"

"I'd known him for less than two days. I wasn't aware of his habits."

"Yet you came here to potentially invest in his school."

Louis blinked, then remembered—he'd told the officer last night about his supposed due diligence. "I'm considering investing. That's different from having already invested."

"Hmm." Arnaud made a note. "There's something else. We found a hair in Charles's office. You'll recall we took DNA samples from everyone last night? The analysis came back remarkably quickly—the benefits of a high-profile case. The hair matches your sample."

Louis's mind went blank for a moment. Then— "Of course my hair might be there. When Hazel screamed, I ran upstairs with Xu Fei. I went into the office, saw what had happened, helped calm Hazel down. I must have lost a hair then."

"You entered the office?"

"Just a step or two. To see what had happened."

"I see." Another note. "Monsieur Bassett, I'm going to be direct. We have circumstantial evidence placing you at the scene. We have a witness claiming to have seen someone matching your description enter the office. We have questions about your timeline that evening. I think it would be beneficial for everyone if you came to the station to discuss this further."

"Are you arresting me?"

"Not at all. This would be voluntary. A chance to clear up these... inconsistencies."

Louis's jaw tightened. "This is ridiculous. You interviewed Priya Patel last night when you found her earring. Why aren't you asking her to come to the station?"

"We're still analyzing the fingerprints on the earring. And on the weapon."

"You won't find my fingerprints on that dagger."

"Why are you so certain?"

"Because I didn't touch it." Louis heard the edge in his own voice, forced himself to calm down. Getting angry would only make him look guilty.

Arnaud studied him for a long moment. "As I said, this would be voluntary. But I strongly encourage you to come. If you're innocent, as you claim, then helping us eliminate you from our inquiries would be beneficial."

The trap was obvious. Refuse and look guilty. Agree and... what? End up in an interrogation room while they built a case on circumstantial evidence and mysterious witnesses?

But what choice did he have?

"Fine," Louis said. "I'll come. But you're making a mistake."

"Perhaps." Arnaud stood. "We'll see."

22

Hazel had been answering the same questions for what felt like forever—where exactly had they gone, what time had they left, who had suggested the trip. She kept glancing across the room where Detective Arnaud was interviewing Louis. Even from a distance, she could see the tension in Louis's shoulders, the way Arnaud leaned forward like a cat who'd spotted prey.

The young officer interviewing her asked another question about the Metro route they'd taken, but Hazel barely heard him. Arnaud was standing now, Louis too. Another officer had joined them.

They were heading for the door.

"Excuse me," she told the young officer. "I need to—"

She was already moving, practically jogging across the entrance hall. "Louis! Wait!"

He turned at the door, and despite everything, he smiled. That easy, charming smile that probably got him whatever he wanted in life. "Ah, my tourist companion. Come to wish me bon voyage?"

"What's happening? Are they arresting you?"

Arnaud's expression tightened. "Monsieur Bassett is voluntarily accompanying us to answer some questions."

"Voluntarily," Louis repeated. "Key word. Apparently they found some circumstantial evidence and a mysterious witness who claims someone matching my devastatingly handsome description was seen entering Charles's office."

"Monsieur Bassett," Arnaud warned.

"What? She asked. I'm being transparent. Isn't that what you want?" Louis's tone was light, but Hazel could see the tension in his shoulders. "Don't worry. This is all a misunderstanding. I'll be back before you know it."

"But—"

"Really." His voice softened. "It's fine. Someone's confused or lying, and we'll sort it out."

Then he was gone, the heavy door closing behind them. Hazel stood staring at it, mind racing. Louis, a murderer? She tried to picture it—those elegant hands wrapping around the dagger, driving it into Charles's chest. The image wouldn't form. But then, what did murderers look like? They probably didn't advertise it with convenient facial tattoos saying "I kill people."

The entrance hall felt smaller without Louis's presence. The other officers were packing up their temporary interview stations, closing notebooks, gathering evidence bags. The young officer who'd been questioning her looked uncomfortable.

"We're finished here for now," he said. "Monsieur Lambert's office will remain sealed during the investigation."

Just like that, they were leaving. As if they hadn't just hauled away one of her... what? Classmates? Friends? The boy she'd been developing an embarrassing crush on despite her better judgment?

Eleanor appeared from somewhere, looking haggard. Her usually perfect appearance showed cracks—hair escaping from her chignon, lipstick worn away. "Well. That was eventful."

The remaining students gathered in a loose circle. Isabella clutched Monique's arm. Sofia stood slightly apart, arms crossed. Priya hadn't even come downstairs. Hiding in her room, maybe, or already packing to leave.

"Classes will resume tomorrow," Eleanor said, visibly pulling herself together. "I know today has been... difficult. I hope you all managed to get some rest despite everything. We'll proceed with the curriculum as planned."

The group dispersed slowly, nobody quite meeting anyone else's eyes. Hazel climbed the stairs with Xu Fei and Yuki, their footsteps echoing in the quiet villa.

"Do you think Louis did it?" Yuki asked when they reached the third floor.

"No," Xu Fei said immediately. "Louis is many things—arrogant, privileged, probably spoiled since birth—but not a killer."

"You've known him for two days," Yuki pointed out.

"Sometimes that's enough."

They paused at their respective doors. Hazel wanted to say something reassuring, but what? Everything will be fine? She didn't believe that herself.

"Tomorrow," she said instead. "We'll deal with tomorrow when it comes."

Inside her room, Hazel collapsed on the bed. Her phone buzzed immediately. Janet.

OMG just saw the news! French pastry school director murdered! Is that YOUR school???

Hazel stared at the message. How had the news traveled to Fillmore already? She started typing a response, then stopped. This was too much for texts. She hit the video call button instead.

Janet answered on the second ring, her face filling the screen. Still in her bakery uniform, flour in her red hair. "Oh my God, Hazel! Are you okay? Are you safe? Should you come home?"

"I'm fine." The lie came automatically. "It's been... complicated."

"Complicated? Girl, someone got murdered! That's not complicated, that's terrifying!"

Hazel found herself laughing despite everything. Trust Janet to cut through to the heart of things. "Okay, yes. Terrifying. But also complicated."

She told Janet everything. Charles recognizing her, the promise to share information about her parents, finding his body. Louis helping with the shock. The investigation. Their tourist afternoon that had felt like escape until the police dragged them back.

"Wait, wait." Janet held up a hand. "Back up. There's a French boy?"

"That's what you focus on?"

"I'm prioritizing. Murder is bad, obviously. But a Frenchman? In Paris? That's like the beginning of every romance novel ever written. This is significant."

"He might be a murderer."

"But is he cute?"

"Janet!"

"What? These are important details. I need the full picture."

Hazel groaned. "Yes. Fine. He's cute. Beautiful, actually. Stupidly, unfairly beautiful. With this voice that makes everything sound like poetry even when he's talking about cheese."

"Cheese?"

"Long story."

"And you think he might have killed Charles."

"I don't know what to think." Hazel pulled her knees to her chest. "The police took him for questioning. There's some witness who claims they saw someone matching his description near Charles's office. But that could be anyone, right? Tall, dark-haired guy in a suit—that's half of Paris."

"Or it could be him."

"Thanks. Super helpful."

Janet's expression softened. "Sorry. I'm trying to be realistic. You don't know these people, Hazel. Any of them could be dangerous."

"I know. And the worst part is Charles was going to tell me about my parents. He knew them, Janet. Actually knew them. And now he's dead and I'll never find out what he wanted to say."

"Unless…"

"Unless what?"

"Unless his death is connected to what he knew."

The thought had been circling Hazel's mind since last night, but hearing Janet say it made it real. "That's crazy."

"Is it? Your parents die in a car accident after transferring a fortune to your grandmother. Twenty-three years later, you show up in Paris and the one person who knew them is murdered hours after promising to tell you the truth? That's a hell of a coincidence."

"So what, you think someone killed Charles to keep him quiet? About something that happened over two decades ago?"

"I don't know. But maybe you should find out."

Hazel laughed, but it came out slightly hysterical. She didn't want to admit she'd already been trying to do exactly that. "Right. Me. A baker from Fillmore investigating a murder in Paris. That makes sense."

"Actually..." Janet's expression turned thoughtful. "I was scrolling through Facebook this morning. Have you heard of Oceanview Cove?"

"No."

"Me neither, until today. It's some seaside town on the East Coast. But apparently they have this retired librarian who solves crimes with his cat. Like, actual murders. There was a whole article about it."

"A librarian and a cat."

"I know it sounds crazy, but apparently they've solved like ten cases. The police actually consult with them now."

"That's the most ridiculous thing I've ever heard."

"More ridiculous than a baker from Fillmore learning French pastry?"

Hazel opened her mouth to argue, then closed it. Janet had a point. Three months ago, she'd been sitting in her empty house, paralyzed by grief and indecision. Now she was in Paris, in a villa that looked like a museum, surrounded by possible murderers.

"Okay, so where do I go from here?" she said finally. "I mean, I've been asking questions, but I feel like I'm just stumbling around in the dark."

"Start with better questions. Who benefits from Charles's death? Who had access to his office? What did he know about your parents that was worth killing for?"

"You've been watching too many crime shows."

"Maybe. But I also know you, Hazel Chase. Once you get an idea in your head, you don't let go. Remember when you decided to perfect that sourdough recipe? You didn't sleep for three days."

"That was different. That was bread."

"This is your parents. That's way more important than bread."

They talked for a few more minutes about safer topics—bakery gossip, Janet's terrible date with the new mailman, how the new girl was working out. Normal things that felt like a lifeline to her old life.

When they hung up, Hazel lay back on the bed, staring at the ceiling.

A retired librarian and a cat solving murders. It was absurd.

But then, if they could do it...

23

Voices from the garden pulled Hazel to the window. Below, three figures stood in a loose circle, cigarette smoke rising in the evening air. Isabella's dramatic gestures were unmistakable even from the third floor. Monique and Sofia flanked her, all three deep in conversation.

They'd been gone last night when Charles was killed. Out clubbing, with dozens of witnesses. The perfect alibi.

Unless it wasn't.

Before she could talk herself out of it, Hazel was moving. Down the stairs, through the entrance hall, out the side door that led to the garden. The evening air was warm, heavy with the scent of roses and cigarette smoke.

"—told him exactly what I thought of his taste in art," Isabella was saying. "Imagine hanging that monstrosity in your bedroom. I don't care how much it cost, ugly is ugly."

"You told your father-in-law his Picasso was ugly?" Monique laughed. "No wonder he hates you."

"It's mutual." Isabella took a drag from her cigarette, then noticed Hazel. "Oh! Our little American. Come to join the exile club?"

"Exile club?"

"Those of us banished to the garden to smoke." Sofia held up her cigarette. "Eleanor made it very clear that smoking inside would result in immediate expulsion. Charles was allergic, apparently."

Was. Past tense. Twenty-four hours and they were already adjusting their grammar.

"I don't smoke," Hazel said. "I just needed some air."

"Smart girl," Sofia said, even as she lit another cigarette. "This is a filthy habit. I quit every January and start again by February."

"At least you make it to February," Monique said. "I usually crack by January third."

"Ladies of great willpower," Isabella laughed. "No wonder we ended up in pastry school. We clearly have excellent self-control around temptation."

They were trying so hard to seem normal, Hazel realized. Making jokes, complaining about ordinary things. But there was a brittleness to it, like they were all playing parts they'd just learned.

"Actually," Hazel said, "I wanted to ask you something. About Louis."

The three women exchanged glances.

"Gorgeous Louis," Isabella sighed. "Arrested for murder. Like something from a film noir."

"He wasn't arrested. Just taken for questioning."

"Same thing," Monique said. "Once the police decide you're guilty, evidence becomes very flexible."

"You sound like you have experience," Sofia observed.

"My second husband had a misunderstanding with the tax authorities. The investigation was... educational."

"Were any of you here when the police were asking questions?" Hazel asked. "Did anyone mention seeing Louis near Charles's office?"

"We weren't here for most of the questioning," Sofia said. "We arrived back just before you and the others. We'd been out sightseeing too—the police had already been working for a while."

"They said they had a witness," Hazel pressed. "Did any of you tell the police about seeing Louis?"

"Why would we?" Monique lit another cigarette. "We didn't see him."

"Someone did. Or claimed to."

"Well, it wasn't us." Isabella's tone had turned defensive. "We were together all night. You can check with the clubs—we made quite an impression, I'm sure."

"Where did you go exactly?"

The three women exchanged glances again. Still getting used to each other, Hazel realized. Still deciding how much to share with virtual strangers thrown together by circumstance.

"Bar Hemingway first," Monique said finally. "At the Ritz. I'd heard about it for years, always wanted to try it."

"The bartender was incredible," Sofia added. "He made me a cocktail based on my personality after talking to me for two minutes. It was perfect."

"Then we went to Babylon," Isabella continued. "Monique knew about it—said it's one of the hottest clubs in Paris right now.

Very loud, very young, very energetic. Not exactly our usual scene, but we were determined to have an adventure."

"What time did you leave here?" Hazel asked.

"You saw us leave the dining room," Isabella said, confused. "Just after ten."

"No, I mean when did you actually leave the villa? The building?"

"Oh. Immediately," Sofia said. "We'd already called a taxi. It was waiting outside the gates."

Hazel studied them. Three women who'd barely known each other twenty-four hours ago, now bound together by being each other's alibis. "Did you know Charles well? Before this week, I mean?"

"Never met him," Isabella said. "I only heard about the school through a friend in Rome who took a course last year."

"Same," Sofia said. "First time I'd heard his name was when I booked the course."

"I knew of him," Monique said. "He had a reputation in certain circles. The kind of chef who could have run any restaurant in Paris but chose to open his own pastry school instead. Some people found that admirable. Others thought he was wasting his talent."

"What did you think?" Hazel asked.

Monique shrugged. "I think people should do what makes them happy. And Charles seemed happy. At least at the banquet. He was proud of this place, you could tell."

"Until someone murdered him," Sofia said quietly.

They fell silent. A breeze stirred the roses, carrying their perfume across the garden. Somewhere in the villa, a clock chimed eight.

"You're very interested in our whereabouts," Monique observed. "Playing detective?"

"Just trying to understand what happened."

"What happened is someone killed Charles." Isabella's voice had gone flat. "In his own office, in his own school. Someone he probably trusted."

"You think it was someone he knew?" Hazel asked.

"Don't be naive. It's always someone you know." Monique blew smoke into the evening air. "Strangers kill for money or thrills. People you know kill for better reasons."

"Like what?"

"Love. Hate. Secrets." Monique's smile was sharp. "The holy trinity of murder."

"Which one applied to Charles?"

"How would we know?" Sofia said. "We'd met him twice. Once when we arrived, once at the banquet."

"He seemed nice," Isabella added. "Charming. Very proper. Very French."

"He was French," Monique pointed out.

"You know what I mean. That particular type of Frenchman who makes you feel underdressed even in couture."

"I liked him," Sofia said quietly. "He was kind when I arrived. I was nervous—stupid, I know, but I was. He made me feel welcome."

"And now he's dead," Monique said. "So much for kindness."

They fell silent again. In the distance, Hazel could hear traffic, the city going about its evening routines. Life continuing despite death, just like Yuki had said.

"The police will check your alibi?" Hazel asked.

"Why?" Isabella's eyes narrowed. "Do you think we're lying?"

"I think everyone's lying about something."

"How very cynical." Monique dropped her cigarette, grinding it under her designer heel. "And probably accurate. But our secrets have nothing to do with Charles's death."

"Then what do they have to do with?"

Monique smiled, that sharp expression again. "If I told you, they wouldn't be secrets, would they?"

"Come on," Sofia said, linking arms with Isabella. "It's getting cold. And I need wine if we're going to spend the evening being interrogated by amateur detectives."

"I'll join you in a moment," Monique said.

The other two left, Isabella's heels clicking on the stone path. Monique waited until they were out of earshot, then turned to Hazel.

"A word of advice? Stop asking questions."

"Why?"

"Because you're not as subtle as you think you are. And because someone in this villa killed Charles. Do you really want them to notice you noticing things?"

"Is that a threat?"

"It's a warning. From someone who's survived three marriages and two suicide attempts." Monique's smile was sad now. "I've learned when to stop pushing. You should too."

She left Hazel alone in the garden, surrounded by the scent of roses and secrets. Above, the villa's windows glowed golden in the gathering dusk. Behind them were students and staff, all with their own reasons for being here.

Someone had killed Charles Lambert. Someone had stolen Hazel's chance to learn the truth about her parents.

If she wanted answers, she'd have to find them herself.

But first, she needed to figure out who was lying.

The problem was, everyone seemed to be lying about something. Or at least hiding something.

The question was whether any of those secrets had anything to do with murder.

24

Hazel woke to soft knocking and the realization that her neck hurt from sleeping in an awkward position. She'd fallen asleep fully dressed on top of the covers, her phone still in her hand. She'd downloaded some murder mystery novel last night thinking she might pick up detective techniques. Instead, she'd fallen asleep three pages in.

"Un moment!" she called, hoping that was right. Her French was getting worse, not better.

She stumbled to the door and found Madame Dubois with the breakfast tray, looking as put-together as always in her black dress. How did some people manage to look professional at—Hazel checked her phone—eight in the morning?

"Good morning, mademoiselle." Madame Dubois bustled in and set the tray on the table by the window. "Classes resume today, yes? You need energy."

The smell of fresh croissants made Hazel's stomach growl. She'd barely eaten yesterday, too wound up from playing detective in the garden. "Thank you. Actually, can I ask—did the police bring Louis back? I noticed his room was quiet."

Madame Dubois's expression tightened slightly. "I have been awake since five o'clock. No police. No Monsieur Bassett."

"Oh." Hazel's stomach did an uncomfortable flip. If they'd kept him overnight, did that mean they'd found something? Or were they just trying to break him down, make him confess to something he didn't do?

She pushed the thought away. Louis was fine. He had to be fine.

"Such a terrible thing," Madame Dubois said. "Poor Monsieur Lambert. And now the school..." She trailed off with a very French shrug that somehow conveyed resignation, sadness, and what-can-you-do all at once.

Hazel seized the opening. "It must be such a shock. How long had you worked for him?"

"Fifteen years. Since the beginning almost." Madame Dubois didn't sound particularly grief-stricken. More like someone discussing a change in bus routes—inconvenient but not devastating.

"You must have known him well."

"One knows what one needs to know." Another shrug. "He was a good employer. Paid on time. Did not make unreasonable demands."

Not exactly a ringing endorsement. Hazel poured herself coffee, trying to look casual. "That night—the night he died—did you notice anything unusual? Hear anything?"

"I was in the kitchen." Madame Dubois's tone suggested this should be obvious. "With Chef Bernard and his assistants. We cleaned after the banquet until almost midnight. Many dishes. Much work."

"All of you together the whole time?"

The housekeeper's eyes sharpened. "You sound like the police, mademoiselle."

"Sorry. I'm just trying to understand what happened."

"What happened is someone killed Monsieur Lambert. Understanding will not bring him back." But then Madame Dubois softened slightly. "But yes, we were together. Gabriel can confirm—he complained the whole time about his girlfriend waiting for him. And Claire was there too, though she spent most of the time on her phone when she thought we weren't looking."

Just like the clubbing trio, Hazel thought. Perfect alibis all around. Everyone accounted for except the people who'd remained in the villa. The loners. Like Priya, who'd fled the dining room angry and upset. Like Eleanor, who'd claimed jet lag. Like Louis, who'd spent an awfully long time helping a drunk woman to her room.

"Well," Hazel said, "I should probably get ready for class."

Madame Dubois nodded and headed for the door, then paused. "Mademoiselle? A word of advice?"

"Yes?"

"In France, we have a saying. *La curiosité est un vilain défaut.* Curiosity is an ugly fault." She gave Hazel a long look. "Sometimes it is better not to know everything."

Then she was gone, leaving Hazel alone with her breakfast and the uncomfortable feeling that everyone in this villa knew she was asking questions.

Time to be more subtle. If that was even possible.

25

Priya's hands shook as she tied her apron. Twelve more days. She just had to survive twelve more days of this nightmare, then she could go home to London and pretend none of this had happened.

Except it had happened. Charles was dead, and she couldn't remember if she'd killed him.

She'd spent another sleepless night trying to force her memory to give up its secrets. She'd even tried some of the meditation techniques Dr. Pearson had taught her, sitting cross-legged on the floor and focusing on her breathing. But the blank space remained stubbornly blank, a black hole where crucial minutes of her life should be.

The demonstration kitchen was already buzzing with conversation when she arrived. Everyone was there—Eleanor in her crisp whites, Chef Rousseau bouncing on his heels with manic energy, the other students clustered in groups. Everyone except Louis.

The relief that flooded through her was almost shameful. With Louis at the police station, she was temporarily off the hook. Maybe they'd found real evidence against him. Maybe he'd confessed. Maybe her nightmare was over and she could finally sleep without wondering if she'd wake up in handcuffs.

"Ah, bon!" Chef Rousseau clapped his hands. "Everyone is here. First, I must say—I am very sorry about Monsieur Lambert. A tragedy. Terrible. But!" He raised a finger. "Eleanor tells me you have voted to continue. This is good. This is what Charles would want. We cook, we learn, we honor his memory with our pastries."

He launched into an introduction of the day's challenge—choux à la crème, cream puffs. Priya tried to focus on his rapid-fire explanation of temperatures and techniques, but her mind kept drifting. Louis at the police station. The blank space in her memory. The way her hands wouldn't stop trembling.

"Partners again, please!" Chef Rousseau announced. "Same as before if possible."

Priya looked for Sofia, expecting to recreate their pairing from the first day. But Sofia was already gravitating toward Isabella and Monique, the three of them moving together like they'd been friends for years instead of days.

The rejection hit harder than it should have. Suddenly she was seven years old again, standing alone on the lacrosse field while teams formed around her. The brown girl nobody wanted on their side.

"Want to partner up?"

Priya spun around. Hazel stood there with a friendly smile that didn't quite hide the calculation in her eyes.

Oh no. She'd heard Hazel in the garden yesterday through her open window, interrogating the others like some sort of amateur detective. And now it was Priya's turn.

But refusing would look suspicious. More suspicious than whatever Hazel might uncover through a few carefully placed questions.

"Sure," Priya said, proud that her voice came out steady. "Though I should warn you, I'm terrible at pastry."

"I'm good enough for both of us." Hazel's smile widened. "I've been making cream puffs since I was twelve."

Eleanor stepped forward, looking harried. "We have uneven numbers with Louis absent. I'll work with Sofia, if that's acceptable?"

Sofia nodded, leaving Isabella and Monique as the final pair. They immediately started whispering to each other, probably gossiping about everyone else.

"Alright!" Chef Rousseau beamed. "To work! Remember—choux pastry is temperamental. It knows when you are afraid!"

Priya followed Hazel to a station, trying not to feel like a lamb being led to slaughter.

They gathered ingredients in relative silence—flour, butter, eggs, more butter. French pastry seemed to involve shocking amounts of butter. Hazel moved with the easy confidence of someone who actually knew what she was doing, measuring with quick precision.

"So," Hazel said casually, cutting butter into cubes, "rough couple of days."

"That's an understatement."

"I keep thinking about that night. About Charles." Hazel's voice was carefully neutral. "You were one of the last people to see him alive, weren't you?"

There it was. The interrogation, starting already.

"I suppose so." Priya focused on cracking eggs, grateful for something to do with her hands. "He followed me when I left the dining room."

"Where did you go? If you don't mind me asking."

Priya had rehearsed this part. "He invited me to his office. To continue our discussion in private."

"And did you go?"

"Yes." No point denying it—her earring had been found there. "We talked for a few minutes, then I went to my room."

"Just talked?" Hazel's tone was still friendly, conversational. Like they were discussing the weather instead of murder.

"Just talked." The lie came easier than Priya expected. "He maintained his position. I maintained mine. We agreed to disagree."

"Did you see anyone else? Hear anything unusual?"

The irony almost made Priya laugh. She couldn't even remember her own actions, let alone what anyone else was doing. "No. The hallway was empty. I went straight to my room."

Hazel nodded, stirring the butter and water in a saucepan. The kitchen filled with the sounds of cooking—whisks against bowls, Chef Rousseau calling out instructions about proper technique, Monique's laughter at something Isabella said.

"Can I ask what the argument was about?" Hazel's voice dropped lower. "I mean, it seemed pretty heated in the dining room."

Priya hesitated. How much truth could she afford to tell? But Hazel would keep digging, and maybe giving her something would satisfy her curiosity.

"It was stupid," Priya said finally. "I didn't really come here to learn pastry."

Hazel's stirring paused for just a moment. "No?"

"I read reviews of the school online. Everyone raved about the food. Not just the pastries—the actual meals. So I looked into it and found out they have an incredible chef here. Bernard something."

"Chef Bernard," Hazel confirmed. "He made that duck at the banquet."

"Exactly. And it was perfect. Restaurant-quality. Better than restaurant-quality." Priya lowered her voice even more. "My restaurant in London—we've been getting complaints. The food is... adequate. But adequate doesn't get you Michelin stars."

"So you came here to poach their chef?"

"To make him an offer." Priya felt heat rise in her cheeks. "I know how it sounds. But I paid for the full course. Fifteen thousand euros just to have a conversation. I thought that would show I was serious."

"What did Chef Bernard say?"

"He was flattered. I offered double his current salary, plus benefits, plus creative control of the menu." Priya measured flour, remembering the chef's shocked expression. "But he said no. Said he was loyal to Charles."

"So you went to Charles."

"I thought maybe if Charles gave his blessing, Bernard would reconsider. I explained that his talent was wasted here, cooking for a handful of people when he could be cooking for thousands. Making a name for himself."

"But Charles said no."

"Charles said absolutely not." The memory of his condescending smile made Priya's jaw clench. "He wouldn't even discuss it. Just kept saying it was 'impossible' and 'inappropriate.'"

Hazel absorbed this, adding flour to her butter mixture. The choux pastry was starting to come together, forming a smooth, glossy ball.

"That must have been frustrating," she said finally.

Priya studied her face, trying to read what she was thinking. "It was. But not worth killing someone over, if that's what you're wondering."

"I wasn't—"

"Yes, you were." Priya surprised herself with the directness. "You've been asking everyone questions. Playing detective. And now you're wondering if I killed Charles because he wouldn't let me hire his chef."

Hazel had the grace to look embarrassed. "I'm just trying to understand what happened."

"Why?"

"Because Louis is sitting in a police station right now, being interrogated for something he might not have done. Because the real killer could be walking around free. Because—" Hazel stopped, seeming to catch herself. "Because it's not right."

The words hit Priya like a physical blow. Louis at the station, detained overnight. Being questioned, pressured, maybe even charged. All while she stood here making cream puffs, not knowing if she was the reason an innocent man might go to prison.

What if she had killed Charles? What if the blank space in her memory hid something unforgivable?

The thought must have shown on her face, because Hazel's expression softened.

"I'm sorry," Hazel said. "I know this is hard for everyone. I didn't mean to—"

"It's fine." Priya forced her attention back to the pastry. "You're right to ask questions. Someone did kill Charles. I just hope the police figure out who before they railroad Louis into a confession."

They worked in silence after that, following Chef Rousseau's instructions. The choux pastry went into the oven. While they waited, they made pastry cream—more eggs, more stirring, more opportunities for Priya's mind to circle back to that blank space in her memory.

What if she never remembered? What if she went her whole life not knowing whether she was capable of murder?

Worse—what if she suddenly remembered while surrounded by witnesses? What if the memory came back and she couldn't hide her reaction?

The cream puffs emerged golden and perfect. Chef Rousseau demonstrated the filling technique, piping cream with practiced precision. Hazel followed his movements exactly, while Priya struggled to control the piping bag.

"You're good at this," Priya said, watching Hazel's cream puffs turn out as professional as the chef's demonstration.

"Practice." Hazel finished the last puff and surveyed their work. "My grandmother insisted on perfection. 'If you're going to do something, do it right.'"

"Sounds like my mother. Except she applied that philosophy to everything. Grades, behavior, appearance." Priya heard the bitterness creep into her voice. "Nothing was ever quite right enough."

"Is that why you opened your own restaurant? Trying to prove her wrong?"

Priya considered this. "Maybe. Or trying to prove her right. I'm not sure there's a difference anymore."

They presented their cream puffs to Chef Rousseau, who pronounced them "Magnifique!" Isabella and Monique had somehow produced lopsided puffs that oozed cream. Xu Fei and Yuki's were technically perfect but boring. Eleanor and Sofia had created an architectural marvel that looked ready for a magazine cover.

"Tomorrow," Chef Rousseau announced, "we make mille-feuille! Very difficult! You will cry!" He seemed delighted by the prospect.

The class dispersed slowly. Priya noticed Hazel hanging back, probably planning to interrogate someone else. The kitchen staff, maybe, or Eleanor. The girl was relentless.

Just like those teachers at Bramley had been relentless, trying to understand what had triggered her "violent outburst" with Rachel and Annie. Just like her parents had been relentless in their disappointment.

Priya touched her ear reflexively—the one that had lost its earring that night. Such a small thing to potentially destroy a life. One piece of jewelry in the wrong place at the wrong time.

She wondered if Louis had been allowed to sleep, or if they'd kept him up all night, wearing him down. She wondered if he'd thought about calling a lawyer.

Most of all, she wondered what was hiding in that blank space in her memory.

And whether she really wanted to know.

26

Hazel watched Priya leave the kitchen, shoulders rigid with tension. The story about trying to hire Chef Bernard made sense on paper, but something still felt off. Like a recipe where all the ingredients were right but the final result tasted wrong.

"Coming to lunch?" Xu Fei appeared at her elbow, already heading for the door.

"In a few minutes. I want to ask Chef Bernard about that duck recipe from the banquet. I'm thinking of trying something similar back home."

Xu Fei gave her a knowing look but didn't comment. Everyone knew Hazel was asking questions by now. Might as well own it.

The kitchen beyond the demonstration area was a different world—industrial and efficient, all stainless steel and purposeful movement. Chef Bernard stood at the pass, wiping down surfaces while his two assistants packaged leftovers.

"Ah, Mademoiselle Chase!" His English was accented but clear. "You come to learn more secrets of French cooking?"

"Your food is incredible," Hazel said honestly. "That duck at the banquet was the best thing I've ever eaten."

"You flatter an old man." But he looked pleased. "Though I am not so old. Forty-five only. In chef years, I am practically a baby."

He was younger than Hazel had expected, with close-cropped gray hair and the powerful forearms of someone who'd spent decades whisking and stirring. His assistants—Gabriel and Claire—continued cleaning with the practiced efficiency of people who'd done this dance a thousand times.

"It must be strange," Hazel said carefully, "continuing on after what happened to Monsieur Lambert."

Bernard's expression darkened. "Very strange. Very sad. Fifteen years I work for him. He gave me my chance when no one else would."

"You were loyal to him."

"Of course. He saved my career. I had some... troubles in my youth. Bad decisions. Other kitchens would not hire me. But Charles, he believed in second chances."

"That's why you turned down the job offer from Priya's restaurant?"

Bernard's eyebrows rose. "She told you about that?"

"She mentioned it. Said you weren't interested despite the money."

"Double salary." Bernard shook his head. "Very generous. But money is not everything. Here, I have routine. Same schedule, same suppliers, same kitchen. In a restaurant?" He made a dismissive gesture. "Chaos. Every night different, never knowing what will come. And the critics! Always watching, always judging. Here, I cook for people who appreciate good food. No stress."

"But now, with Charles gone..."

"Yes." Bernard's hands stilled on the counter. "Now I wonder if I was foolish. Eleanor is good, but she is not Charles. The school may not survive. Perhaps I should have taken Madame Patel's offer."

"You still could. If the school closes."

"Perhaps. Or perhaps I am too old to start over. Gabriel here"—he nodded toward the younger assistant—"he has ambitions. Wants his own restaurant one day. Maybe he should be the one to go to London."

Gabriel looked up from the sink, startled. "Chef?"

"Just thinking aloud." Bernard waved him back to work. "Tell me, mademoiselle, why these questions? You are not a detective."

"No. Just trying to understand what happened."

"What happened is someone killed a good man. Understanding the why will not bring him back."

The same thing Madame Dubois had said, almost word for word. Hazel wondered if the staff had discussed it among themselves, agreed on a party line.

"The police seem to think Louis Bassett did it," she said.

Bernard snorted. "The police think what is convenient. Young man with no alibi? Easy target. But I saw Monsieur Bassett at dinner. He does not have the eyes of a killer."

"What do killer's eyes look like?"

"Empty. I have seen them, in my troubled youth. Men who could hurt you and feel nothing." He shuddered slightly. "Monsieur Bassett's eyes are not empty. Arrogant, perhaps. Amused by his own cleverness. But not empty."

"Then who?"

Bernard spread his hands. "I am a chef, not a detective. I was here, washing dishes with Gabriel and Claire and Madame Dubois. We heard nothing, saw nothing. The first we knew of trouble was when the police arrived."

More perfect alibis. Everyone accounted for except the people who mattered.

"The cleaning is finished," Claire announced, pulling off her apron. "Shall we go serve lunch now?"

"Yes, go." Bernard turned back to Hazel. "You will eat? I made bouillabaisse. Good for the soul after tragedy."

Hazel's stomach growled on cue. "That sounds wonderful."

She followed them to the dining room, mind churning. Priya's story checked out, but it also gave her a motive—if the school closed, Chef Bernard might reconsider her offer. Was that enough to kill for? It seemed like a long shot, literally gambling someone's life on a maybe.

But then, people had killed for less.

Hazel needed to talk to Eleanor. About the school's future, about her movements that night. About whether she'd wanted Charles's job enough to take it by force.

27

Eleanor picked at her bouillabaisse, barely tasting Chef Bernard's excellent cooking. Around her, the students chatted in small groups—Isabella regaling Monique with a story about Rome Fashion Week, Xu Fei showing Hazel something on her phone, Yuki listening to Sofia describe Swedish winters.

Only Priya sat alone, stirring her soup without eating. She looked exhausted, purple shadows under her eyes like bruises.

They were all pretending, Eleanor realized. Playing at normalcy while Charles's blood was barely dry. Yesterday she'd moved through the villa in a fog of grief and duty, making necessary phone calls, dealing with police, reassuring panicked investors. Today the fog had lifted, leaving behind a crushing weight of memory.

Charles hiring her when she was nobody—just another American with pastry dreams and decent French. Their first catastrophic event when the ovens had broken an hour before a visiting dignitary arrived. Charles in the kitchen at 3 AM, teaching her how to temper chocolate because *"one must always keep learning, Eleanor."*

The way he'd take off his glasses when concentrating, leaving red marks on his nose. His terrible jokes that only he found funny. The secret stash of supermarket cookies in his desk drawer because sometimes even master pastry chefs wanted processed sugar.

Fifteen years of partnership, of building something beautiful together, ended by someone in this villa.

"Are you alright?"

Eleanor startled. The dining room had emptied while she'd been lost in memory. Only Hazel remained, studying her with those observant eyes.

"I was just thinking." Eleanor straightened, trying to pull her professional mask back into place. "About Charles. About what happens now."

"May I?" Hazel gestured to the chair beside her.

"Of course."

They sat in silence for a moment. Through the windows, Eleanor could see the garden where Charles had loved to walk in the evenings, planning new courses, dreaming of expansion.

"I've been wondering," Hazel said carefully, "what this means for the school. Long-term."

"I wish I knew." The words came out more bitter than Eleanor intended. "Charles handled the business side—the investors, the marketing, the grand vision. I just assisted with teaching and managed day-to-day operations."

"You must have picked up some of it. Fifteen years is a long time."

"You'd think so. But Charles had a gift for making people believe in him. When he walked into a room, investors reached for their checkbooks. When I walk in…" Eleanor shrugged. "They see the deputy. The assistant. The woman who was good enough to support but not to lead."

"That's their loss."

"Maybe. Or maybe they're right. Maybe I'm not suited for this."

Hazel tilted her head. "Did you want it? The director position?"

The question Charles himself had asked, years ago, when he'd been drawing up succession plans. *If something happens to me, Eleanor, the school becomes yours. Would you want that?*

She'd laughed it off then. Charles was healthy, vital, going to live forever.

"I don't know," Eleanor admitted. "I never wanted the spotlight. I was happy being the power behind the throne, making sure everything ran smoothly while Charles charmed the world. Now…" She gestured at the empty room. "Now I have to be both."

"About that night," Hazel said, the transition so smooth Eleanor almost missed it. "You left right after Isabella, Monique, and Sofia went clubbing?"

Ah. So this was why Hazel had stayed behind. Not concern for Eleanor's wellbeing, but more questions. More investigation. Part of Eleanor wanted to be offended. The rest was oddly impressed.

"Straight to my room," she confirmed. "I wasn't lying about jet lag. Barely made it up the stairs."

"You didn't hear anything? Your room must be on the same floor as Charles's office."

"At the end of the corridor. The villa's bigger than it looks—sound doesn't carry well. I took a sleeping pill and was out until the screaming woke me."

Your screaming, she didn't add. That horrible sound that had announced the end of everything.

"No one can verify that," Hazel observed.

"No." Eleanor met her gaze steadily. "They can't. Which I suppose makes me a suspect. The ambitious deputy who wanted the top job."

"I didn't say that."

"You didn't have to." Eleanor surprised herself with a laugh. "You're not as subtle as you think, Hazel. Half the villa knows you're playing detective. The other half is too self-absorbed to notice."

Hazel flushed. "I'm just trying to—"

"Find the truth. I know. And I appreciate it, actually. The police seem fixated on Louis, but I can't see him killing Charles. Too much effort for someone who treated life like a game."

"You think someone else did it."

"Obviously someone else did it. The question is who." Eleanor leaned back, decision made. If Hazel wanted to investigate, why not give her some actual facts? "Would you like some information that might help?"

Hazel's eyes sharpened. "What kind of information?"

"I spoke with Villa security yesterday. Professional courtesy—they were very helpful once they understood I wasn't trying to make their lives difficult. The entrance gate cameras confirmed Isabella, Monique, and Sofia left before Charles died. Left and didn't return until after the police arrived."

"So they're clear."

"Completely. The timing doesn't work unless they have teleportation powers." Eleanor watched understanding dawn on Hazel's face. "Which narrows our suspect list considerably."

"What about cameras inside the villa?" Hazel asked. "I haven't noticed any, but maybe they're hidden?"

Eleanor shook her head. "Charles was particular about that. He wanted the school to feel like stepping back in time—no security cameras, no key cards, nothing that would spoil the atmosphere. 'If we can't trust our students,' he used to say, 'we shouldn't be teaching them.'"

"That seems…" Hazel searched for words. "Optimistic."

"Charles was an optimist. He believed in people. Look where it got him." Her voice turned bitter. "There's only one camera—at the main entrance, facing outward to see who's approaching. Security confirmed nobody entered or left except our clubbing trio."

"What about other exits? Fire doors?"

"All checked. All locked from the inside, untouched." Eleanor let the implications sink in. "The killer was already here. Is almost certainly still here."

28

Hazel's temples throbbed as she sank onto the wooden bench in the gazebo. The structure sat at the far edge of the garden, half-hidden by climbing roses that had been carefully trained along its latticed walls. Pink and white blooms cascaded in deliberate abundance, their scent almost cloying in the afternoon heat. From here, the villa looked smaller, less imposing. Just a big house full of secrets and possible murderers.

She pressed her fingers against her forehead, trying to organize the chaos of information swirling in her brain. Every conversation from the past two days felt significant now, every glance potentially meaningful. The problem was separating real clues from the paranoid imaginings of someone who'd stumbled into their first murder investigation.

The clubbing trio—Isabella, Monique, and Sofia—were supposedly clear. Security cameras confirmed they'd left before Charles died and hadn't returned until after. Unless they'd somehow teleported back, murdered Charles, and teleported out again. Which seemed unlikely, even for wealthy Europeans who probably had resources Hazel couldn't imagine. Still, the way they'd moved together, like a unit already, made her wonder what else they might be keeping to themselves.

Eleanor had opportunity but what motive? Fifteen years as deputy director, content to stay in Charles's shadow. Or was she? Maybe that contentment had curdled into resentment over the years. Maybe she'd grown tired of being the power behind the throne, watching Charles take credit for work they'd done together. The way she'd talked about investors seeing her as "just" the assistant—there was real bitterness there.

But Eleanor seemed genuinely devastated by Charles's death, those tears in the entrance hall too raw to be performance. Then again, guilt could look a lot like grief. Hazel had seen that at her grandmother's funeral, distant relatives weeping hardest who'd never visited when Bridget was alive.

Priya's story made more sense now. Coming here to poach Chef Bernard, getting shut down by Charles. The argument, the trip to his office, the missing earring. Everything pointed to her. Maybe too neatly. Real life was messier than mystery novels, where clues lined up like dominoes waiting to fall. In real life, evidence was contradictory, witnesses unreliable, and sometimes there were no satisfying answers.

Then there was Louis. Beautiful, charming Louis who'd spent an awfully long time helping drunk Yuki to her room. Hazel's mind kept circling back to that gap in time. What took so long? Yuki had been drunk but not unconscious. The third floor wasn't that far. Unless—

The thought crept in before she could stop it. What if they'd—no. Hazel cut off that thought, but it crawled back anyway. What if he'd taken advantage of Yuki's condition? The idea made her stomach turn. She'd rather believe he was a murderer than that he'd—

Stop. She was letting her imagination run wild. Yuki had seemed fine the next morning. Tired and hungover, but not traumatized. Not moving with the careful distance of someone who'd been violated. Just two people navigating stairs while one of them could barely walk. Hazel had helped enough drunk friends to know it really could take forever, especially if they kept stopping to avoid being sick.

Even Madame Dubois crossed Hazel's mind, though the housekeeper had the best alibi of all. In the kitchen with three witnesses, cleaning up after the banquet. Unless they were all lying for each other, which seemed like a conspiracy too far.

And somewhere in this mess lay the truth about her parents. Charles had known them. Had theories about the money, about their deaths. Those theories that might explain why two young people would transfer a fortune to an elderly woman and then die in a car accident days later. Now those secrets were lost forever, taken to the grave by whoever wielded that dagger.

Unless they weren't. Unless Charles had written something down, kept records. But where? His office was sealed, and even if she could get in, what would she look for? A file marked "Secret Information About the Chases"? Life wasn't that convenient.

How did fictional detectives do this? Miss Marple would have spotted some tiny detail by now—a misplaced button or suspicious gardening tool that revealed everything. Hercule Poirot would have gathered everyone in the drawing room and explained exactly how the crime unfolded, each revelation building to an inevitable conclusion. But Hazel was just a baker from Fillmore with a headache and too many questions.

She closed her eyes, letting her mind drift back. Memory had a way of offering unexpected connections when you stopped trying to force them.

She'd been twelve, maybe thirteen. Sunday after church, the ladies auxiliary setting up for their monthly potluck. The social hall had smelled like casseroles and judgment, the particular combination that Hazel associated with church functions. Mrs. Carpenter's prized charm bracelet—silver with little dangling hearts—had gone missing from her purse in the coat room.

Hazel, fresh off a Pretty Little Liars binge, had appointed herself lead investigator. She'd even made a notebook specifically for the case, drawing a magnifying glass on the cover with colored pencils.

She'd questioned everyone with the confidence only a preteen could muster. Who'd been near the coat room? Who needed money? Who had admired the bracelet? The church ladies had humored her, answering questions while hiding smiles behind their hands. Even then, Hazel had noticed how different people reacted to questions—some eager to help, others defensive even when innocent, a few enjoying the drama of it all.

Then Monday at school, Ashley Carpenter had cornered Hazel by the lockers. Her face was blotchy from crying, eyes red-rimmed and desperate.

"I need to tell someone," she'd whispered, glancing around to make sure the hallway was empty. "I took Grandma's bracelet. I needed money for—" She'd broken off, but later Hazel learned it was for concert tickets. Some boy band that Ashley was convinced would change her life if she could just see them perform. She'd planned to pawn the bracelet, buy the tickets, then figure out how to buy it back before anyone noticed.

Thirteen years old and willing to steal from her grandmother for a chance to see five boys sing about teenage love.

The truth had been hiding in plain sight. The granddaughter who'd sat through Hazel's interrogation at the potluck, probably dying inside with every question. Who'd even suggested other suspects, trying to throw Hazel off the trail.

But guilt had its own weight. Ashley couldn't carry it, had to confess to someone, and somehow Hazel—the amateur detective who'd made everything worse—had seemed like the safest option.

Footsteps on gravel pulled Hazel from the memory. Someone was walking across the garden toward her, shoes crunching on the path with measured steps. The gait was both hesitant and determined—an impossible combination that somehow made perfect sense when Priya came into view.

She looked worse than she had in class that morning. The composure she'd maintained while making cream puffs had completely dissolved. Her usually immaculate appearance had crumbled—hair that had been perfectly styled now hung limp around her face. The designer clothes had been replaced with faded jeans and a button-down shirt that looked like she'd grabbed it from the floor.

"I was looking for you," Priya said, stopping a few feet from the gazebo. Her voice was steady but thin, like she was holding herself together through sheer will. "We need to talk."

29

Hazel straightened on the bench, studying Priya's face. The woman looked exhausted beyond what a single sleepless night could cause. The dark circles under her eyes had deepened since morning, and her hands trembled slightly at her sides. Whatever she wanted to say, she'd been building up to it for a while.

"Okay," Hazel said carefully. "Want to sit?"

Priya moved like her bones hurt, each step deliberate and painful. She settled on the opposite end of the bench, as far from Hazel as possible while still sharing the same seat. For a moment, she just stared at the villa, seeming to gather courage from the view of its solid walls.

"I've been thinking about what you said." Priya's voice was steady but quiet, like she was afraid of being overheard even out here. "About Louis sitting in a police station for something he might not have done."

She paused, picking at a loose thread on her jeans. "You're the only one asking real questions. Not just gossiping or speculating, but actually trying to understand. You deserve to know what happened. Or at least, what I remember happening."

Hazel waited. Sometimes silence drew out more truth than questions. She'd learned that at the bakery, letting difficult customers talk themselves out while she boxed up their orders.

"The argument in the dining room—you saw that." Priya's jaw tightened at the memory. "Charles was so dismissive. Like I was some silly woman with too much money and not enough sense. Some bored housewife playing at business."

Her voice took on an edge. "I've built my restaurant from nothing. Fought for every review, every customer, every inch of respect in an industry that still thinks women belong in pastry kitchens making pretty desserts. And Charles sat there, sipping his wine, explaining why my proposal was 'inappropriate.'"

"That must have been frustrating."

"Frustrating." Priya laughed, short and bitter. "I left because I could feel it building. The anger. I've learned to recognize the signs—the way my vision starts to narrow, how sounds get both louder and more distant. Like standing in a tunnel with a train coming."

"The signs of what?"

Priya finally looked at her, and the fear in her eyes made Hazel's chest tight.

"I have... episodes. Blackouts, I guess you'd call them. When I get angry enough, I just—" Priya made a helpless gesture. "Blank. Like someone hits a switch and I'm gone. When I come back, sometimes minutes have passed. Sometimes longer."

The pieces clicked together in Hazel's mind. The nervous touching of her ear during interviews. The exhaustion that went beyond simple lack of sleep. The fear behind her composed facade. She'd been carrying this secret, wondering what she might have done in those missing minutes.

"It started at boarding school," Priya continued, her voice taking on the flat quality of someone recounting an old trauma. "Bramley Hall. Forty thousand pounds a year to be tormented by girls named Rachel and Annie."

She picked harder at the thread, unraveling the seam of her jeans. "They were clever about it. Never anything obvious when teachers were around. Just constant, subtle reminders that I didn't belong. Comments about curry smell. Jokes about hygiene. Asking if my parents owned a corner shop."

Hazel thought of her own school experiences in Fillmore. She'd been lucky—too insignificant to be a target, too poor to be a threat. She'd floated through, neither popular nor unpopular, just there.

"One day they cornered me in the second-floor bathroom." Priya's eyes went distant. "Rachel blocked the door while Annie went on about how we'd all noticed the smell in the dorm room. How even Matron had mentioned it. Lies, of course. But effective."

"What happened?"

"I don't know." The words came out raw. "One moment I was standing at the sink, rage building like pressure in a kettle. The next, I was being pulled off Annie by a horrified teacher. Both girls on the floor. Rachel's nose bleeding. Annie with scratches down her cheek."

Just like Ashley Carpenter, Hazel thought. Confessing because the weight of the secret was crushing her. But this was different. Ashley had known what she'd done. Priya was confessing to a blank space, a possibility.

"It happened a few more times over the years," Priya continued. "Always when someone pushed exactly the right buttons. University was better—people were more mature, less cruel. But occasionally..."

She trailed off, lost in memories Hazel could only imagine.

"I got therapy, learned coping mechanisms. Breathing exercises. Meditation. Ways to recognize the build-up and remove myself from situations. I hadn't had an episode in five years." Priya's laugh was bitter. "Then that night at the banquet happened."

"You left the dining room angry."

"I had to get out. I could feel it building. But Charles followed me into the hallway." Priya's voice tightened at the memory. "He caught up with me, all concerned and reasonable. 'Let's discuss this in my office,' he said. 'Perhaps we can find a compromise.'"

She stood abruptly, pacing to the gazebo entrance and back. The movement seemed to help her focus.

"So I went to his office. Stupid, I know. But I thought maybe away from the others, he'd see reason. Understand that I was offering Chef Bernard an opportunity, not trying to steal him."

Hazel waited, letting Priya find her own pace.

"He sat behind his desk, poured himself wine from that special bottle he kept—1982 something, he made sure to mention the year. Didn't offer me any, of course. Then he explained, very patiently, like I was a child who'd misbehaved, why my proposal was impossible."

Hazel could picture it perfectly. Charles in his element, probably enjoying his power to dismiss Priya's offer. The same man who'd promised to tell her about her parents, who'd seemed so kind and generous. Everyone had different faces.

"I tried to stay calm. Explained again about the opportunities for Chef Bernard, the money, the prestige of working in London."

Priya's hands clenched into fists. "Charles just kept smiling that condescending smile. 'My dear,' he said, 'some things are more important than money. Loyalty, for instance. Honor. Concepts that perhaps are foreign in the restaurant business.'"

"That's when it happened? The blank space?"

"I remember the rage hitting me. That familiar tunnel vision starting. My hands shaking." Priya pressed her palms against her eyes. "Then—nothing. Next clear memory is being in my room, touching my ear and finding the earring gone."

She turned to face Hazel fully, and the fear in her eyes was terrible. "What if I killed him? What if I grabbed that dagger and—" She couldn't finish. "In my other episodes, I hurt people but never... never anything permanent. But I was so angry, Hazel. Angrier than I'd been in years. What if I finally crossed that line?"

Hazel thought of Ashley Carpenter again, thirteen and terrified, confessing to theft because she couldn't carry the secret alone. But this was bigger than a stolen bracelet. This was murder. And Priya wasn't confessing to a crime—she was confessing to the possibility of one.

"Priya," Hazel said carefully, "do you know anything about Charles knowing my parents?"

Confusion replaced fear on Priya's face. "Your parents? No, I—what do you mean?"

Hazel hesitated. But Priya had been honest with her, had trusted her with a secret that could destroy her life. The least she could do was return the favor.

"Charles knew my parents at university. They died when I was two—car accident. But before that, they transferred a fortune to my grandmother. No one knows where the money came from or why they did it." The words came easier than expected, worn smooth by repetition in her mind. "Charles recognized me that first night. Said I looked exactly like my mother. He promised to tell me what he knew, had theories about the money and their deaths. He seemed urgent about it, like it was important I know. But then…"

"Oh God." Priya's face crumpled like paper. "If I killed him—if I took that chance away from you—"

"We don't know what happened yet."

"Don't we?" Priya's laugh had an edge of hysteria. "My earring in his office. These blackouts where I've hurt people before. A history of violence when triggered. It all points one way."

She sank back onto the bench, seeming to shrink into herself. "I'm so sorry. If I really did this—if my anger stole your chance to learn about your parents—I don't know how to live with that."

"You need to tell the police," Hazel said gently. "About the blackouts, about everything. They have Louis—"

"You're right." Priya straightened, seeming to find some resolve. "I'll tell them. They need the full picture. Whatever happens, at least Louis won't suffer for my—for whatever I did. He doesn't deserve that."

She paused, her face crumpling with another wave of guilt. "There's something else. When they questioned me about my earring, I panicked. I was so scared, not thinking straight. They asked if I'd seen anyone near Charles's office that night, and I—" Her voice broke. "I told them I saw someone matching Louis's description going in. I didn't actually see anyone. I just… I was terrified and it came out."

Hazel felt her stomach drop. "You lied about Louis being there?"

"I know how awful it sounds. I wasn't trying to frame him specifically—I didn't even really know him. I just blurted out a description of someone tall, dark-haired. Generic enough." Priya pressed her hands against her face. "God, what kind of person does that? He's sitting in a police station right now because of my lie. Because I was a coward."

Hazel's mind raced. Part of her wanted to be angry—Louis was being interrogated because of this lie. But looking at Priya's devastated face, she mostly felt sad. Fear made people do terrible things.

"You need to tell them that too," Hazel said quietly. "The whole truth. Right away."

"I will. I'll tell them everything—the blackouts, the lie, all of it." Priya's voice was steadier now, resolved. "Maybe then they'll let him go. Thank you for listening. For not... judging me too harshly."

"Thank you for telling me this. It couldn't have been easy."

"Easier than carrying it alone." Priya managed a weak smile. "You're a good listener, Hazel. Your grandmother raised you well."

The mention of Bridget made Hazel's throat tight. She would have known what to say right now, how to comfort someone facing something terrible.

"Madame Patel!"

They both turned. Madame Dubois stood at the garden door, slightly out of breath. Her usually perfect appearance showed signs of haste—a strand of gray hair escaping from her bun, her hands smoothing her black dress nervously.

"There you are," the housekeeper said, relief evident in her voice. "The police have returned. They are looking for you."

30

Priya's first thought was absurd—had the police bugged the garden? Were they listening to her confession to Hazel? But no, that was paranoid. They couldn't have arrived so quickly even if they had been listening. This was something else. Something that had nothing to do with her decision to confess.

Which somehow made it worse.

She followed Madame Dubois back through the villa, Hazel close behind. Each step felt heavy, like walking through water. Her legs didn't want to work properly, muscle memory failing under the weight of dread. At least she wouldn't have to carry the secret anymore. She'd tell Detective Arnaud about the blackouts, about the missing time. Maybe they could piece together what she couldn't remember.

Or maybe they already had.

The entrance hall was crowded with uniforms. More officers than before, their presence filling the space with official authority. Detective Arnaud stood near the stairs, looking even more tired than yesterday. The lines around his eyes had deepened, and his suit looked like he'd slept in it. But it was the figure beside him that made Priya's step falter.

Louis. Looking exhausted, his usually perfect hair disheveled, his clothes wrinkled. But very much not in custody. He stood slightly apart from the police, like a man who'd been through an ordeal and come out the other side.

Relief flooded through her, followed immediately by confusion. If they'd released Louis, then why—

"Ah, Madame Patel." Arnaud's voice was professionally neutral, giving nothing away. "We need you to accompany us to the station. If you would come voluntarily, it would be appreciated. Otherwise…"

He didn't need to finish. The threat of handcuffs, of being dragged out like a criminal, hung in the air.

"I'll come." The words felt distant, like someone else was speaking. Her voice sounded calm, reasonable. Inside, her heart hammered against her ribs. "No need for dramatics."

Movement on the stairs caught her eye. The other students were gathering—Isabella and Monique at the top, leaning against the banister like spectators at a show. Sofia and Yuki halfway down, more cautious in their curiosity. Xu Fei peered around the corner, camera notably absent for once. Eleanor appeared from the second-floor hallway, face carefully composed but eyes sharp with concern.

All of them watching Priya like she was a stranger. Or a murderer.

Only Hazel's eyes held understanding. She knew about the blackouts now, about the possibility that Priya might have done something unforgivable and not even remember it.

An officer gestured toward the door. Young, probably new, with the kind of eager efficiency that hadn't yet been worn down by the job. Priya walked on legs that didn't feel like her own, each step an effort of will.

The police car waited outside, back door open like a mouth ready to swallow her whole. The vinyl seat felt hard and unwelcoming through her jeans, the space smaller than she'd expected. It smelled like disinfectant and fear—how many people had sat here, knowing their lives were about to change?

"Why are you taking me to the station?" she asked.

The officer in the driver's seat shrugged without turning around. "I... no speak English," he said in a thick accent.

Of course he didn't. Because this was France, and she was just another foreigner who'd gotten herself into trouble.

They waited in silence that stretched like taffy. Through the window, she could see the others still watching from the entrance hall. The scene felt surreal, like something from one of those true crime shows her mother loved. Except she was living it.

Detective Arnaud climbed in beside her, bringing the smell of cigarettes and bitter coffee. He said something to the driver in French, and the car pulled away from the villa. Through the gates, Priya could see the crowd of reporters surge forward, cameras flashing like strobes. Someone pounded on the window, shouting questions in French and accented English.

"Ignore them," Arnaud said, though he looked annoyed himself. "Parasites."

Once they'd cleared the media gauntlet and reached the relative quiet of regular Paris traffic, he turned to her.

"We've analyzed the fingerprints," he said without preamble. "Both from your earring and from the weapon."

Priya's mouth went dry. She'd known this was coming, had been preparing for it, but the reality still hit like a physical blow. "And?"

"They match." He watched her face carefully, those pale eyes missing nothing. "They belong to you."

The world tilted. Everything she'd feared, confirmed in those simple words. If her fingerprints were on the dagger, then she'd held it. If she'd held it during her blackout, then she'd—

Oh God. She'd actually done it. Killed Charles in one of her blank rages. Let Louis spend a night in police custody for her crime. Stolen Hazel's chance to learn about her parents. Everything she'd worked to control, all those years of therapy and careful management, destroyed in a moment she couldn't even remember.

She could hear Dr. Pearson's voice in her head: *"The anger isn't wrong, Priya. It's what we do with it that matters."* But she'd done the worst possible thing with it.

"I hope," Arnaud said, his voice cutting through her spiral, "you have some explanation for those fingerprints."

Priya stared at her hands—murderer's hands now—and sighed. The weight of it all, the terrible possibility of what she'd done, pressed down on her chest.

"I'm afraid my explanation will only raise more questions."

31

Louis's expression remained neutral as Detective Arnaud apologized again for the inconvenience. Twenty-four hours in custody, treated like a criminal, and all he got was "inconvenience" and tight smiles that didn't reach anyone's eyes.

"You were doing your job," Louis said. "No hard feelings."

Arnaud looked relieved. Probably worried about lawyers and lawsuits. He had reason to worry, but Louis had no intention of making waves.

The entrance to the villa felt different after a night in the station. Smaller somehow, less grand. Or maybe he was just exhausted. They'd kept him up most of the night, tag-team interrogations in a room that smelled like old cigarettes and desperation. The same questions over and over, looking for cracks in his story. Different officers with different approaches—one sympathetic, one aggressive, one who barely spoke and just stared with unnerving intensity.

Madame Dubois appeared from a side hallway, walking with—

Priya. Looking like death warmed over, but trying to maintain some dignity. Her shoulders were straight but her face was haggard, like she'd aged years in days.

Louis felt genuine sympathy for her. They were about to do to her what they'd done to him. Hours of questions, accusations, trying to force a confession. The poor woman had no idea what she was in for. The way they'd wear her down, use her own words against her, make her doubt her own memory.

More uniforms filed in. The entrance hall was getting crowded. Louis noticed how they positioned themselves—blocking exits without being obvious about it. Professional. Practiced.

"We need you to accompany us to the station," Arnaud told Priya.

Priya agreed to go voluntarily, saving herself the indignity of handcuffs. Louis watched her walk to the door, shoulders straight but defeat in every line of her body. He knew that feeling—the moment when you realized you were trapped in the machinery of justice, guilty or not.

Behind him, footsteps on the stairs—the vultures gathering to watch the show. He could feel their eyes, their curiosity. Everyone loved drama when it wasn't happening to them.

When the police car pulled away, everyone turned to him. Isabella, Monique, Sofia, Yuki, Xu Fei, Eleanor. All wanting answers, wanting gossip, wanting to know what happened. He could see the questions forming, the hunger for details.

And Hazel. Looking at him with those wide eyes, concern written across her face.

"What happened?" Eleanor asked, her professional composure cracking slightly. "Why did they take Priya?"

"I overheard them talking." His voice was heavy with exhaustion—twenty-four hours of interrogation would do that to anyone. "They found fingerprints. On the weapon and on her earring. Both Priya's."

Isabella made a satisfied noise. "I knew it. That missing earring—it was obvious from the start. I said so, didn't I, Monique?"

"You said a lot of things," Monique murmured, but she was watching Louis with sharp eyes.

"Nothing's obvious," Hazel said, an edge to her voice. She turned to Louis, expression softening. "How are you, Louis? Are you okay?"

He met her eyes and smiled.

"They tried their best to get a confession." He rubbed his face. "Asked the same questions fifty different ways. 'Where were you?' 'What did you see?' 'Why did it take so long?' But I couldn't confess to something I didn't do."

"The conditions must have been awful," Hazel said.

"Not the Ritz, that's certain. Barely slept. The coffee tasted like motor oil and the breakfast—" He shuddered. "Let's just say I have new appreciation for Chef Bernard. I may never complain about overcooked eggs again."

That got a few smiles and scattered laughter. The tension in the room eased slightly as people remembered the mundane complaints of everyday life.

"But you're eager to continue tomorrow?" Eleanor asked. "The course, I mean? After everything?"

"Of course." He straightened. "Charles would want us to continue. He was so proud of this place. And frankly, after the food at the station, I need Chef Rousseau's pastries more than ever.

You haven't lived until you've tried to choke down stale bread that might have been fresh sometime last week."

More laughs. The tension breaking. People starting to drift away, the show over. Isabella murmuring something to Monique about needing wine. Sofia checking her phone. The normal rhythms of life reasserting themselves.

"I'm glad you're okay," Hazel said quietly when they were alone in the entrance hall. "I was worried. We all were."

"Were you?" His voice was warm. "That's very sweet."

She flushed slightly. "I just—I knew you didn't do it. It didn't feel right. You're not..." She paused, searching for words. "You're not someone who could kill another person."

"Your instincts were good." He touched her arm lightly, briefly. Enough to make a connection, not enough to seem forward. "Thank you for believing in me. It means more than you know."

Her smile was worth the risk of connection. Open, honest, without artifice. When was the last time someone had smiled at him like that? Without wanting something, without calculation?

"Get some rest," she said. "You look exhausted. Actually exhausted, not just French-movie exhausted."

"Planning on it. Twelve hours minimum. Maybe thirteen if I'm feeling indulgent."

He headed for the stairs, moving slowly. The adrenaline that had kept him going through the interrogation was fading, leaving behind a bone-deep weariness. His hand gripped the banister, pulling himself up like an old man.

His room was exactly as he'd left it. Bed still made, books still arranged on the shelf. For a moment he just stood in the doorway, taking in the familiar space. After twenty-four hours of concrete walls and metal furniture, the elegant room felt almost surreal.

Louis sank onto the bed, not bothering to remove his shoes. The relief hit him all at once—he was free. Actually free. No more questions, no more suspicious stares, no more implications that he was hiding something. The police had Priya now, and whatever happened next, he was clear.

His mind drifted to Hazel. The way she'd looked at him downstairs, that mix of concern and something else. Relief? Affection? She'd believed in him when the evidence looked bad, kept faith when others doubted. That meant something.

What exactly did he feel for her? It was hard to tell anymore what was real and what was just the intensity of the situation. Trauma had a way of creating bonds that might not exist under normal circumstances. She was beautiful, yes, and kind. That combination of strength and vulnerability that made her interesting to watch.

When she'd smiled at him downstairs, when she'd said she was glad he was okay, something in his chest had loosened. Maybe it was just gratitude. Maybe it was something more. He was too tired to analyze it now.

Louis closed his eyes, letting his body sink into the mattress. Tomorrow he'd have to face everyone again. Deal with the awkwardness of being the suspected-then-cleared student. But that was tomorrow's problem.

For now, he could just breathe. The weight that had been pressing on his shoulders for the past day finally lifted. He was free, Hazel believed in him, and life would go on.

Whatever happened next, at least this part was over.

32

The croissants emerged from the oven golden and perfect, their layers separating in delicate spirals that caught the morning light. Hazel watched Louis attempt to transfer them to the cooling rack, his movements still awkward but improving. Three days had passed since Priya was taken away, and the villa had settled into an unsettling normalcy that made Hazel's skin itch.

"Like this," she said, demonstrating the proper wrist rotation. "Quick and confident. If you hesitate, they'll know."

"The croissants will know I'm afraid of them?" Louis raised an eyebrow.

"Pastry always knows." She kept her voice light, matching the mood that had descended on the school. Nobody mentioned Charles anymore. Nobody talked about Priya sitting in police custody, possibly for a crime she didn't remember committing. The students attended classes, made perfect choux and delicate mille-feuille, and pretended murder hadn't touched their lives.

Chef Rousseau bounced between stations, correcting techniques with his usual enthusiasm. "Non, non! The butter must be cold! Always cold! You want layers, not mush!"

Isabella laughed at something Monique whispered. Sofia worked with focused precision. Xu Fei documented everything for her millions of followers. Life went on, as if death was just a minor inconvenience to be swept under expensive Persian rugs.

"Your croissants are getting better," Hazel told Louis as they cleaned their station. "That last batch almost looked professional."

"Almost?" He clutched his chest in mock offense. "I'll have you know I'm considering opening my own patisserie. 'Louis's Almost Professional Croissants.'"

"Catchy."

The afternoon brought another of Louis's tours through hidden Paris. Today he'd promised to show them a secret garden that most tourists never found, tucked behind an unmarked door in the Marais. Yuki and Xu Fei joined them, cameras ready.

Paris revealed itself differently through Louis's eyes. Not the postcard city of monuments and museums, but a living place with stories in every stone. He knew which bakery made the best pain aux raisins. He could tell you why certain buildings had bullet holes from the war, carefully preserved. He made the city feel like a friend sharing secrets.

"My grandfather used to bring me here," Louis said, pushing open a wooden door that looked like it led to someone's storage shed. Instead, they found themselves in a courtyard garden, wild roses climbing ancient walls, a fountain bubbling in the center. "He said every Parisian needed a place to hide from the world."

Xu Fei immediately started photographing, murmuring about light quality. Yuki sat on a stone bench, face tilted toward the sun. Hazel found herself watching Louis as he explained the garden's history—how it had survived the Revolution, hidden behind its unmarked door.

She was in trouble. Each day brought new reasons to like him. The way he listened when she talked about her grandmother. How he'd started bringing her coffee exactly how she liked it during their morning classes. The self-deprecating jokes when his pastries failed spectacularly.

"You're thinking too hard," he said, appearing beside her. "I can actually see the gears turning."

"Just enjoying the garden."

"Liar." But his smile was gentle. "You get this little line right here", he almost touched the space between her eyebrows, "when something's bothering you."

The fact that he'd noticed made her stomach flip. "It's nothing."

"Is it about Priya?"

How did he always know? Maybe because she'd been obviously distracted for days, staring into space during Chef Rousseau's demonstrations, burning sugar because her mind was elsewhere.

"I can't stop thinking about it," she admitted. "Her confession about the blackouts. What if she didn't actually—"

"The police found her fingerprints on the weapon." His voice was gentle but firm. "Sometimes the obvious answer is the right one."

"I know. You're right." But the doubt remained, a stone in her shoe she couldn't shake loose. Priya's terror had been real. Her confusion about those missing minutes genuine. What if the blackout had given someone else an opportunity? What if—

"Come on," Louis said, taking her elbow. "Let me show you the best ice cream in Paris. Guaranteed to cure overthinking."

She let him lead her through winding streets, tried to lose herself in his stories about student protests and midnight adventures. But two thoughts circled her mind like hungry sharks.

Priya might be innocent.

And Charles had taken answers about her parents to his grave.

That night, Hazel lay in bed staring at the ceiling. The police had unsealed Charles's office yesterday. She'd overheard Eleanor telling Madame Dubois that she'd deal with his personal effects after the course ended. But for now, the office sat empty, full of whatever secrets Charles had kept.

The photograph. He'd specifically mentioned a photograph he wanted to show her. If it existed, if it was still there, it might hold some clue about her parents. About why they'd transferred a fortune days before dying. About what Charles's theories had been.

The idea was insane. Breaking into a dead man's office to search for clues like some discount Nancy Drew. But the alternative was never knowing, and that felt worse than any risk.

Before she could talk herself out of it, Hazel made a decision. Tonight, after everyone was asleep, she'd search Charles's office. She'd find that photograph or confirm it didn't exist. Either way, she'd have an answer.

The clock on her nightstand glowed: 11:47 PM.

Soon.

33

Hazel had changed into dark jeans and a black sweater, feeling ridiculous. She wasn't a cat burglar. She was a baker who sometimes burned cookies. But here she was, easing her door open at 12:13 AM, wincing at every tiny sound.

The hallway stretched before her, dimly lit by wall sconces turned low for the night. She'd mapped the route in her head—down to the second floor, turn left, first door on the right. Simple. Except the villa had apparently been constructed entirely of squeaky floorboards and her feet seemed magnetically attracted to every single one.

Creeeeak.

She froze. Nothing. Just the settling sounds old buildings made, probably. She took another step.

CREEEEAK.

Jesus. She might as well announce her criminal intentions over a bullhorn. "Attention everyone, Hazel Chase is about to commit breaking and entering. Please remain in your rooms."

Shadows shifted at the edge of her vision. She spun around—nothing. Just her imagination painting threats where none existed. Get it together, she told herself. You're sneaking around a pastry school, not infiltrating the CIA.

The marble stairs presented a new challenge. Each step threatened to announce her presence with sharp clicks. She hugged the wall, placing her feet carefully at the edges where the stone met the wall. Halfway down, her phone vibrated in her pocket.

The buzz might as well have been a fire alarm. She fumbled for it, heart hammering, and saw a text from Janet.

How's Paris? Saw another article about the murder!

Not now, Janet. Hazel switched the phone to silent and shoved it deep in her pocket.

The second-floor hallway was darker, only one sconce still glowing. Charles's office door loomed ahead, looking exactly like it had that night. Her hand hesitated on the doorknob. Last time she'd touched this door, she'd found—

No. Don't think about that. Think about answers. Think about the photograph.

The door opened silently. Thank God for small mercies and well-oiled hinges. She slipped inside and closed it behind her, then stood in the darkness, letting her eyes adjust.

The office looked different in the shadows. Moonlight through tall windows painted everything in shades of gray. The desk squatted in the center like a patient animal. The chair behind it was empty now, but her mind supplied the image anyway—Charles sitting there, the dagger handle protruding from his chest.

She shook her head hard, banishing the memory. Focus. She was here for a reason.

Hazel pulled out her phone and switched on the flashlight, keeping the beam low. The office was neater than she'd expected. Either Charles had been naturally organized or someone had already been through his things. She started with the obvious places—desk surface, bookshelf, the credenza against the wall. Nothing that looked like a treasured photograph.

The desk drawers were more promising. Top drawer: pens, paperclips, the detritus of office life. Second drawer: files labeled in French she couldn't read, what looked like financial documents. Third drawer: locked.

Her pulse quickened. Of course. If Charles had something precious, something personal, he'd keep it locked away. The drawer was solid wood with an old-fashioned lock, the kind that took a proper key rather than a combination.

She could probably force it. Find something to pry with, accept the damage as collateral. But that would leave evidence of her break-in, and Eleanor would definitely notice a destroyed drawer when she came to sort through Charles's things.

Keys. Where would he keep keys?

She ran the flashlight over the desk again, then remembered—the morning after the murder, the police cataloging evidence. They'd been meticulous about potential weapons but less concerned with ordinary objects.

There. On a small hook behind the desk lamp, almost invisible unless you were looking for it. A ring of keys, various sizes. One was clearly for the office door, too large for the drawer. Another looked like a house key. But the third...

The small brass key slid into the lock like it belonged there. Which it did. The drawer opened with a soft click that sounded like victory.

Inside, beneath various documents and what looked like personal correspondence, she found it. A silver frame, face-down, the kind of weight that suggested quality. Hazel lifted it carefully and turned it over.

Four people smiled at the camera, young and impossibly alive. An old university building rose behind them, beautiful in that timeless way of academic architecture. Charles stood on the left, recognizable despite the decades—same sharp features, same confident posture, just wrapped in smoother skin and darker hair.

But it was the couple in the middle that made Hazel's throat tight. Her parents. She'd seen photos, of course, the few her grandmother had kept. But those had been formal portraits, stiff and staged. This was different. Her mother laughed at something, head thrown back, joy radiating from every line. Her father had his arm around her, looking at her instead of the camera, his expression soft with the kind of love that made other people uncomfortable.

They looked so young. So unaware that in a few years they'd be dead, leaving behind a confused fortune and a daughter who would grow up wondering.

The fourth person was a woman Hazel didn't recognize. Pretty in that delicate way that suggested good breeding and careful maintenance. She stood slightly apart from the others, smiling but not quite matching their easy intimacy.

This woman might know something. Might have answers about her parents that Charles had taken to his grave. Hazel had to find her.

A floorboard creaked in the hallway.

Hazel's hand jerked, nearly dropping the photograph. She clicked off the flashlight instantly, plunging the room into darkness. Her heart hammered against her ribs.

Another creak, closer. Deliberate. Someone was moving carefully, just as she had, trying to be quiet.

Oh God. What if it was the real killer? What if they'd come back for something, evidence they'd left behind? What if—

The doorknob began to turn.

Hazel set the photograph on the desk and positioned herself beside the door. Her grandmother's voice echoed in her head: *"Surprise is your best advantage. Strike first, ask questions later."*

The door opened slowly. A figure stepped through, barely visible in the darkness.

34

Hazel didn't think. Her body moved on muscle memory, all those self-defense classes her grandmother had insisted on suddenly useful. She grabbed the intruder's arm, pivoted her hip, and used their momentum against them. A classic hip throw, executed perfectly.

The intruder hit the floor with a thud and a very French curse. "Merde! Qu'est-ce que—"

She knew that voice. Hazel straddled the prone figure, one hand pinning their wrist, the other fumbling for her phone. The flashlight beam revealed Louis's shocked face staring up at her.

"Louis? What the hell are you doing here?"

"I could ask you the same thing." His voice was strained but amused. "Where did you learn to do that?"

"Self-defense classes." She was suddenly very aware that she was sitting on top of him, their faces inches apart in the darkness. "My grandmother made me take them."

"Your grandmother was a wise woman." He shifted slightly beneath her. "Though I'm beginning to question her motivations."

Her grandmother had been paranoid about safety. Always. Double-checking locks, insisting Hazel call when she arrived anywhere, jumping at unexpected sounds. She'd enrolled Hazel in self-defense at age ten, ignoring protests that it wasn't ladylike.

"I don't want to fight," ten-year-old Hazel had whined. "I want to bake."

"You can do both," Bridget had said firmly. "But only one might save your life someday."

Hazel had been good at it. Better than good. By the time she graduated high school, after eight years of weekly classes, she could take down men twice her size. The instructor had tried to recruit her for competitions, but Hazel preferred her kitchen to the gym. Still, the skills remained, apparently.

"You haven't answered my question," she said. "What are you doing here?"

"I went to the kitchen for a late snack. Chef Bernard left some éclairs that were calling my name." His breath was warm against her face. "On my way back, I saw light under the door. Thought I should investigate. And now here I am, defeated by someone half my size."

"I'm not that small."

"No," he agreed, eyes dropping to where she still straddled him. "You're not."

She realized she was still pinning his wrist and released it, but didn't move from her position. The air between them shifted, awareness crackling like electricity. His hands had somehow found her waist, steadying her. Or maybe holding her there.

Her heart was racing for entirely different reasons now.

"This is..." she started.

"Unexpected?"

"I was going to say awkward."

"That too." But he didn't look awkward. He looked like a man exactly where he wanted to be. "Not that I'm complaining, but perhaps we could continue this conversation in a more conventional position?"

Heat flooded her face. She scrambled off him, nearly tripping in her haste. He sat up slowly, rubbing his shoulder.

"Remind me never to startle you," he said. "My ego can only take so much."

"Sorry. I thought you might be—" She stopped. *Thought you might be the real killer* sounded paranoid even in her head.

"The murderer returning to the scene?" He stood, brushing dust from his jeans. "Very dramatic. Very American thriller novel."

"Something like that."

He studied her in the dim light. "So what are you really doing here, Hazel? And please don't say you were craving éclairs too."

She hesitated. Trust came hard when someone had been murdered feet from where they stood. But Louis had been nothing but kind these past days. He'd been cleared by the police. And she needed someone to know, in case—

In case what? In case she ended up dead like her parents?

"Charles knew my parents," she said finally. "At university. He recognized me that first night, said I looked exactly like my mother."

Something flashed across Louis's face. Surprise? Concern? It was gone before she could identify it.

"He promised to tell me about them," she continued. "Said he had theories about things. About why they died, where their money came from. He was going to show me a photograph after the banquet, but—"

"But someone killed him first." Louis finished quietly.

"Yes." The word came out bitter. "And now I'll never know what he wanted to tell me."

"So you broke in to look for answers. Find anything?"

She retrieved the photograph from the desk, angling it so he could see. He leaned close, his shoulder brushing hers.

"Your parents?"

She nodded, pointing them out. "And Charles. But I don't know who she is." Her finger hovered over the unknown woman.

"They look so happy together." His voice was soft, studying her parents. "No wonder they had such a beautiful daughter."

Heat crept up her neck. "Louis—"

"Sorry. Inappropriate timing." But his smile suggested he wasn't sorry at all. "Have you considered showing this to Eleanor? Or Madame Dubois? They knew Charles better than anyone."

"The photo's from university. Years before they met him." She slipped the frame into her bag. "Besides, how would I explain where I got it? 'Oh, I just happened to be rifling through Charles's locked drawers in the middle of the night'?"

"Fair point. Though you could always lie. You seem to have hidden depths."

"I'm a terrible liar."

"Also a fair point." He glanced around the office. "We should go. The longer we stay, the more likely someone catches us. And while I'm sure you could take them down too, it might raise questions."

She followed him to the door, then stopped. "Why are you being so calm about this? I basically broke into a crime scene."

"Technically, the police released it. So it's just regular breaking and entering." He opened the door, checking the hallway. "Besides, I understand wanting answers about your past. We all have our ghosts."

They made their way back through the villa, keeping to the shadows. The floorboards seemed quieter now, or maybe she just cared less about the noise.

"I could help," Louis offered as they climbed the stairs. "Finding the woman in the photograph."

"No." The refusal came out sharper than intended. "I mean, thank you, but I don't want to drag you into my family drama. You've dealt with enough lately."

He shrugged, that particularly French gesture that could mean anything. "The offer stands. Though I hope our future meetings won't involve quite so much violence."

"Only if you behave," she said, attempting lightness.

"I'll do my best." They'd reached the third floor. "Don't stay up too late searching. Someone needs to keep me from burning croissants tomorrow."

"Chef Rousseau would never forgive me."

"Exactly. The fate of French pastry rests in your capable, violent hands."

She watched him disappear into his room, then slipped into her own. The photograph sat heavy in her bag, four young faces frozen in time. One dead. Two dead. One unknown.

But not for long. Hazel had found the photograph. Now she just needed to find the woman.

35

Hazel spread the photograph on her desk and took a picture with her phone. The quality wasn't great—her hands shook slightly, and the desk lamp created glare on the glass—but it would have to do.

Google's image search was her first attempt. She cropped the photo to show just the unknown woman and uploaded it, waiting for the magic of technology to provide answers.

The results were useless. Random women who looked nothing like her target. Stock photos of "young professional woman" and "university student smiling." Google's algorithm couldn't account for decades of aging, for how faces changed while bone structure remained.

She needed someone better with computers. Someone who understood the dark arts of digital investigation.

Mike Santos.

Her stomach twisted at the thought. They'd been friends since middle school, bonding over a shared love of vintage video games and silly comedies. He'd helped her through calculus, she'd taught him to make chocolate chip cookies. Easy friendship, uncomplicated by romance.

Until it wasn't.

But Mike was her best shot. He worked at The Tech Spot on Ventura Street now, fixing computers and probably hacking government databases for fun. He'd know how to find someone from an old photograph.

If he'd talk to her. Which, given that he'd blocked her number, email, and every form of social media, seemed unlikely.

She checked the time. 12:47 AM in Paris meant 3:47 PM in California. The bakery would be closed by now. Janet would be finishing up the cleaning, probably eating leftover pastries and complaining about her diet.

The phone rang twice before Janet answered. "Please tell me you're calling to say you've fallen in love with a French count and need me to be your maid of honor."

"No counts. Sorry to disappoint."

"What about that Louis guy? Still suspicious?"

"He's—" Hazel thought about their encounter in Charles's office. "It's complicated."

"The best things usually are. So what's up? It's got to be late there."

"I need a favor. A big one."

"Hit me."

"I need you to talk to Mike Santos. Ask him to unblock me."

Silence. Then: "Oh, honey. Are you sure that's a good idea?"

"I know he hates me. But I need his help with something important."

"Hate's a strong word. I think 'devastated' is more accurate."

Hazel winced. She'd handled that whole situation badly, but how was she supposed to know Mike's feelings ran so deep? They'd been friends. Just friends. At least, that's what she'd thought.

"It's about my parents," she said. "I found a photograph. Someone who might have known them. But I need help tracking her down, and Mike's the only person I know who could do it."

"Playing the dead parents card. Harsh but effective." Janet sighed. "I'll try. But if he sets my hair on fire with his computer lasers or whatever, you're paying for the reconstructive surgery."

"He doesn't have computer lasers."

"You don't know what that boy's invented since you broke his heart."

"I didn't—" Hazel stopped. No point relitigating the past. "Just tell him it's important. Please."

"Fine. I'm leaving now anyway. The Tech Spot's on my way home." Another sigh. "You owe me so many croissants for this."

"All the croissants. Forever."

"Damn right."

Hazel spent the next twenty minutes pretending to read, checking her phone every thirty seconds. When it finally rang, she nearly dropped it in her eagerness.

"Okay, that was awkward," Janet said without preamble. "He literally tried to hide behind a computer monitor when he saw me."

"But?"

"But I cornered him by the printers and explained the situation. Told him about the murder, about your parents, about the photograph. Laid it on thick."

"And?"

"He'll do it. Not for you, he made that very clear about sixteen times. But for the mystery. Apparently, he's been bored fixing suburban malware infections."

Relief flooded through her. "Thank you. Thank you so much."

"He said to send the photo on WhatsApp. And Hazel? Maybe keep it professional. The boy's still pretty raw."

"I will. I promise."

They hung up, and Hazel immediately opened WhatsApp. Her last messages to Mike sat there with single gray checkmarks—sent but not delivered, blocked before they could reach him.

She typed carefully: *Mike, thank you for agreeing to help. I'm sorry again about everything. The woman I need to find is the one on the right in this photo.*

She attached the image and hit send. The gray checkmark appeared. Her chest tightened. What if he'd changed his mind? What if—

The second checkmark appeared. Delivered.

Seconds later, they turned blue. Read.

A thumbs up emoji appeared.

It wasn't much. A single emoji, the bare minimum of communication. But from someone who'd blocked her everywhere, it felt like progress.

Hazel set the phone aside and finally let exhaustion wash over her. She'd broken into a dead man's office, been tackled by (and then tackled) Louis, and possibly rebuilt a bridge she'd carelessly burned.

Tomorrow there would be croissants to make and mysteries to solve. But tonight, she'd done what she could.

The photograph lay on her desk, four faces smiling at a future they couldn't see coming. Somewhere out there, the fourth person might be living a quiet life, unaware that a baker from California was about to come looking for answers.

Hazel turned off the light and crawled into bed. She checked her phone one more time, hoping maybe Mike had already found something. But no—just that single thumbs up emoji staring back at her.

Still, Mike was the best at what he did. If anyone could track down a person from a decades-old photograph, it was him.

She just had to be patient.

36

Hazel's phone screen glowed in the morning darkness. 7:45 AM. She squinted at WhatsApp, hoping for something more than that single thumbs up emoji from Mike. Nothing. The emoji stared back at her, unchanged from last night.

Was he already working on it? Or was this his revenge—making her wait, letting her stew in uncertainty? Mike could be petty when he wanted to be. She remembered the time in tenth grade when she'd beaten him at Mortal Kombat. He'd spent the next week "accidentally" spoiling every TV show she was watching.

Her fingers hovered over the keyboard. Maybe just a quick message to check in? No. That would look desperate. Impatient. Everything Mike probably thought she was anyway. Let him work at his own pace. She'd waited long enough for answers. A few more days wouldn't kill her.

The shower helped clear her head, steam and heat chasing away the lingering exhaustion from her midnight adventure. She kept thinking about Louis in Charles's office, the weight of him beneath her, the way his hands had found her waist. Professional, Hazel. Keep it professional.

She pulled on her usual class outfit—jeans that had seen better days, a t-shirt that wouldn't show flour too badly, the same sneakers she'd worn to death. Not exactly Parisian chic, but she was here to learn, not to win fashion awards.

The demonstration kitchen already buzzed with pre-class energy when she arrived. Xu Fei was setting up her cameras at the perfect angle to catch the morning light. Yuki stood at her station, ingredients already measured out with military precision. The clubbing trio huddled together, probably comparing hangover remedies.

"Any luck with your search?"

Louis appeared at her elbow, looking unfairly good for someone who'd been thrown to the floor eight hours ago. His casual button-down was perfectly pressed, his hair perfectly tousled. Did French people wake up camera-ready?

"Not yet." She busied herself with tying her apron. "These things take time."

"Offer still stands. I might be able to help."

"My friend's a genius with computers. He'll find her." The word "friend" tasted bitter. Was Mike still her friend? Could you be friends with someone who'd blocked you on every platform known to man?

Louis studied her face for a moment, then seemed to come to a decision. "You need a distraction. Come to the Louvre with me this afternoon."

"The Louvre?" She couldn't hide her surprise. "I already checked. Last admission is at five, and the lines—we'd never make it after class."

"I have a friend who works there. She can get us in without the queue."

She. Of course it was a she. Probably some elegant French woman who spoke four languages and never burned croissants.

"That sounds lovely!" Monique's voice cut through whatever Hazel had been about to say. "I haven't been since my school days. Mind if I join? I'd love to see how it's changed."

Louis's expression flickered—annoyance? disappointment?—before settling into polite resignation. "Of course."

"The Louvre?" Isabella perked up from beside Monique. "I'm coming too. I need to see if that hideous portrait my mother-in-law donated is still on display."

"Count me in," Sofia added. "I should probably see it at least once while I'm here."

Within minutes, the entire class had invited themselves along. Even Eleanor, overhearing the commotion, smiled at their enthusiasm.

"You absolutely should go," she said. "No one should leave Paris without visiting the Louvre. Chef Rousseau and I will prep tomorrow's lesson while you're gone—you deserve an afternoon of culture after all your hard work."

"I suppose my friend can arrange a group visit," Louis said, his tone suggesting he'd rather arrange a root canal.

Hazel caught his expression—the same one he'd worn that first day when Xu Fei had invited herself on their Metro adventure. Had he been trying to ask her on a date? The thought sent an unexpected flutter through her stomach.

Well, she thought, at least the Louvre would keep her mind off that thumbs up emoji burning a hole in her phone.

37

The crowds outside the Louvre made Times Square look deserted. Tourists moved in slow-motion herds, following guides with colored flags held high like battle standards. The line for tickets stretched around the courtyard, a snake of humanity baking in the afternoon sun.

Hazel tugged at her dress—a simple blue sundress that had looked better in her room than it did surrounded by actual Parisians. She'd even put on makeup, more effort than she usually made. Purely because they were going to a museum. Not because Louis had said she looked lovely when they'd gathered in the entrance hall.

"Most of these people won't even make it in," Sofia observed, checking her watch. "Two hours until closing."

"But we will," Louis said with the confidence of someone who'd never waited in line for anything. "Ah, there's Céleste."

A woman detached herself from the museum entrance and walked toward them. Of course she was beautiful. Of course she moved like a dancer. Of course she greeted Louis with kisses on both cheeks that lasted a beat too long.

"Louis! Ça fait longtemps." Her English, when she switched for the group's benefit, was perfect. "And these are your friends from the pastry school?"

She wore the kind of simple black dress that whispered money in every perfectly placed seam. Her hair was pulled back in an effortless chignon that Hazel couldn't achieve with an hour and a can of hairspray.

"Thank you for accommodating us," Yuki said politely. "I know it's a lot to ask."

"For Louis? Anything." Céleste's smile was warm, but her eyes lingered on him in a way that made Hazel's jaw clench. "Come, I'll take you through the group entrance. Part of an educational tour—no one will question it."

She led them past the snaking lines, through a side door marked "Groupes Scolaires." The security guard nodded at Céleste, barely glancing at their ragtag bunch of pastry students trying to look educational.

"Your friends will want to start with the Italian paintings," Céleste told Louis, her hand brushing his arm. "I'll leave you to explore. Bonne visite!"

More cheek kisses. More lingering. More of Hazel trying not to care.

"So," Monique said when Céleste had click-clacked away on her perfect heels, "how does one become friends with Louvre employees?"

Louis shrugged. "We dated for a while. Years ago. Still friends."

Dated. The word sat heavy in Hazel's stomach. She found herself cataloguing the differences between herself and Céleste. The French woman was all elegance and sophistication. Hazel was a baker who occasionally tackled men in dark offices.

"She seems nice," Yuki said diplomatically.

"She is," Louis agreed, already moving toward the galleries. "Now, who wants to fight through crowds to glimpse the Mona Lisa?"

The Louvre, Hazel discovered, was like Disneyland for art lovers. If Disneyland were designed by someone with a sadistic sense of humor and no concept of crowd control.

"Move back! S'il vous plaît, move back!" A guard gestured frantically as Xu Fei, walking backward to get the perfect shot of a ceiling fresco, crashed directly into a German tourist the size of a small building.

Xu Fei squeaked something in Chinese that sounded distinctly like profanity, her camera swinging dangerously close to a priceless vase.

"This way to the Mona Lisa!" Isabella called, consulting her phone map. She turned left confidently. "Or wait, is that right?"

"We've lost Yuki," Sofia reported. "She was just here—"

"I'm here!" Yuki's voice came from behind a massive tour group of Japanese seniors. "Got swept away by my people!"

They moved through the galleries like a dysfunctional school trip. Isabella kept stopping to take selfies with statues, making increasingly ridiculous faces. Monique provided running commentary on which artists had the most scandalous personal lives. Xu Fei documented everything, occasionally walking into walls when she forgot to look where she was going.

"And this," Monique announced loudly in front of a nude statue, "is exactly the ass my personal trainer promised me. Where do I file a complaint?"

"Madame!" A guard materialized from nowhere. "S'il vous plaît, lower your voice!"

"She's right though," Isabella stage-whispered. "That is a spectacular—"

"MADAME!"

Hazel and Louis exchanged looks and quietly distanced themselves from the group.

"They're going to get us thrown out," Hazel muttered.

"Probably. Want to see the Mona Lisa before that happens?"

The Mona Lisa room was a zoo. Hundreds of people crammed against barriers, phones held high, trying to capture the world's most famous smile. The painting itself, behind bulletproof glass and what looked like every security measure short of attack dogs, was surprisingly small.

"That's it?" Hazel stood on her tiptoes, trying to see over a wall of shoulders. "It's so... tiny."

"Disappointing?" Louis asked.

"No. Just... I expected it to be bigger. Grander. Something that justified all this." She gestured at the crowds. "But it's just a woman with a weird smile in a box."

"The French tourism board would have you executed for that opinion."

"Good thing I'm American. We're expected to have bad taste."

They navigated through more galleries, Louis pointing out his favorites with an enthusiasm that made Hazel smile. He knew stories about the artists, scandals behind the paintings, which pieces had been stolen and recovered. The museum came alive through his eyes.

"How do you know all this?" she asked as they paused before a massive canvas depicting Napoleon's coronation.

"My best friend's father worked here as a curator. Before Céleste, he was my connection." His voice softened. "He used to sneak us in after hours sometimes. Just us and all this art. Made me feel like I owned the place."

"That must have been magical."

"It was." He pointed to a massive painting of a battle scene. "I used to pretend I was leading the charge. Nearly knocked over a statue once, playing war."

They'd circled back to where the others were gathered around the Venus de Milo. Xu Fei was practically vibrating with excitement, trying to get the perfect angle. Sofia was reading the placard aloud. Isabella and Monique were making increasingly inappropriate comparisons to their yoga instructor.

And Hazel, transfixed by the marble perfection, stepped closer. The way the light hit the ancient stone made it seem almost alive, like the goddess might step down from her pedestal at any moment. The crowds pressed behind her, someone's elbow digging into her back. She moved forward to escape, just wanting to see the intricate carving of the drapery, the way it seemed to flow like real fabric. Her hand moved without conscious thought, reaching toward the smooth surface—

BEEP BEEP BEEP BEEP!

The alarm shrieked through the gallery. Red lights flashed. A voice boomed from hidden speakers: "SECURITY ALERT! PLEASE STEP AWAY FROM THE ARTIFACTS!"

Every eye in the room turned to Hazel, her hand frozen inches from the statue. The German tourist from earlier shook his head disapprovingly. A child pointed and laughed. Someone was definitely filming this.

"I didn't—I wasn't—" Heat flooded her face. "I'm sorry!"

The guard who'd been watching them throughout their visit finally had enough. He spoke rapidly in French to his colleague, then approached their group with the expression of someone whose patience had completely evaporated.

38

"You must leave now," the guard said in careful English, though his tone made it clear this wasn't a request. "All of you. Please follow me to the exit."

Hazel's face still burned as they emerged into the evening air. The sun was setting, painting the sky in shades of embarrassment that matched her cheeks.

"Well," Monique said cheerfully, "that was more exciting than my last visit. Though slightly less educational."

"I can't believe I set off an alarm." Hazel covered her face with her hands. "At the Louvre. I'm going to be banned from France."

"Nonsense," Sofia said. "This happens more than you'd think. The guards see worse every day."

"Remember when that woman climbed into the fountain?" Monique added helpfully. "Or when those teenagers tried to recreate the Raft of the Medusa? You barely registered on the scandal scale."

"Besides," Louis said quietly, just for her, "you should see your face when you're caught doing something wrong. Absolutely adorable."

Before Hazel could process that, Isabella clapped her hands. "Right! The night's young and we're already ejected from cultural activities. Bar?"

"Bar!" Monique agreed. "I need wine to process all that culture."

"One drink," Yuki said. "Classes tomorrow."

"You sound like Eleanor," Monique laughed. "Next you'll be reminding us about proper knife technique."

They found a bar three blocks away, the kind of place that looked like it had been serving wine since Napoleon was in short pants. Dark wood, dim lighting, the smell of centuries of spilled drinks and whispered secrets. A long table in the back accommodated their group perfectly.

"I'll get the first round," Louis offered. "Hazel? Xu Fei? Help me carry?"

The bar was three-deep with after-work drinkers. Hazel squeezed in beside Louis, trying to catch the bartender's eye. The French system of bar service remained a mystery—there seemed to be no queue, just whoever could project the most confidence.

"Excusez-moi, love." The voice was British, pure boarding school privilege. "Couldn't help but notice you from across the way."

Hazel turned. The man was handsome in that specific way of British men who'd never been told no—floppy hair, pink cheeks, the slight glaze of too many drinks.

"Oh. Um. Thanks?"

"Fancy joining me and the lads?" He gestured toward a table of similar specimens. "We're celebrating Nigel's promotion. Loads of champagne. Pretty girl like you should have champagne."

"That's very nice, but—"

Louis's hand found hers, fingers interlacing naturally. "I don't think you noticed she's with someone." His voice had an edge Hazel hadn't heard before, something protective and possessive that made her pulse jump.

British Boy's eyes tracked down to their joined hands, then back up to Louis's face. Something in Louis's expression made him take a half-step back.

"Right. Sorry, mate. No offense meant." He retreated to his table with the careful movements of someone who'd just realized he'd poked the wrong bear.

Hazel's hand tingled where Louis held it. They stood frozen for a moment, the contact electric. His thumb brushed over her knuckles, just once, before the spell broke.

The bartender appeared, sliding drinks across the bar with a stream of rapid French that Hazel couldn't follow.

Xu Fei's smile could have powered the Eiffel Tower. "That was very smooth. Both of you."

"We should probably…" Hazel gestured vaguely toward their table, very aware that Louis still hadn't let go of her hand.

"Right. Drinks."

They managed to transport everything without dropping any glasses, though Hazel's hands shook slightly. From the almost-confrontation. Not from Louis defending her honor like some kind of modern knight. Definitely not from the way he'd said "she's with someone" like he meant it.

"Truth or dare!" Monique announced once everyone had drinks. "We're not too old for drinking games, are we?"

"Apparently not," Yuki said, but she was smiling.

"I'll start." Monique's eyes gleamed with mischief. "Hazel. Truth or dare?"

"Truth."

"That day in the garden—did you really think we were murderers?"

Hazel felt the table's attention focus on her. "I suspected everyone at first. But that evening, I also got the feeling you were all hiding something else. You even said your secrets had nothing to do with Charles's death."

The three women exchanged glances. Isabella sighed.

"Fine. You want our secrets? That whole thing about the course being a birthday gift from my husband? Complete lie." She took a large sip of wine. "I paid for it myself. Found out three weeks ago he's been having an affair. With his secretary, because apparently we're living in a bad cliché."

"Isabella," Sofia said softly.

"No, it's fine. I'm here deciding if I want to save my marriage or burn it to the ground. Leaning toward arson, if we're being honest."

"I'll bring matches," Monique offered. "My first husband cheated. The divorce was spectacular."

"Since we're confessing," Sofia said, "I wasn't entirely truthful either. I didn't take a sabbatical from the Foreign Ministry. I was fired."

"Fired?" Yuki looked shocked.

"I accidentally seated the Finnish ambassador's wife next to the Norwegian cultural attaché at a state dinner. Turns out they'd had an affair three years ago. She threw her soup at him. He threw his wine at her. The Swedish foreign minister got caught in the crossfire. Beet soup all over his white tie." Sofia grimaced. "International incident might be putting it mildly."

"That's amazing," Isabella breathed.

"Not according to my boss. But then I met Erik—he's in tech, too much money, not enough sense—and he insisted I follow my passion. Paid for the course and everything. Said life's too short to arrange seating charts."

"My reasons for coming were true," Monique said. "Recently divorced, fabulously single, all that. But I may have forgotten to mention that my ex-husband doesn't know I'm still in Paris. Told him I was at a spa in Switzerland with no phone service. If François knew I was here, he'd manufacture some crisis requiring my immediate return. Anything to avoid actually parenting our son alone."

"That's brilliant," Isabella said.

"It's necessary." Monique turned to Louis. "Your turn, darling. Taking an expensive pastry course for a New Year's resolution? Please. What's the real reason?"

Louis shrugged. "I told Hazel already. I'm considering investing in the school. Wanted to see if it lived up to its reputation."

"Still considering it?" Sofia asked. "Given recent events?"

"Why not? If Eleanor continues with the school, she'll need investors. Tragedy doesn't erase potential."

"Did you study business at university?" Yuki asked. "For the investing?"

"Political science, actually. Sorbonne. Very tedious—should have done something more practical."

Hazel frowned. She was almost certain he'd mentioned Oxford when they first met. Something about cooking being a survival skill there. The wine must be affecting her memory.

"Most embarrassing romantic moment?" Xu Fei asked Hazel when her turn came.

Hazel groaned. "Pass?"

"No passing!" the table chorused.

"Fine. I once wrote a love poem to my crush and accidentally turned it in as my English homework. My teacher read it to the entire class as an example of 'overly purple prose.'"

The table erupted in sympathetic groans.

"That's horrible," Yuki said. "Mine is worse though. University, second year. I had a massive crush on this American exchange student in my statistics class. Finally worked up the courage to confess my feelings after months of pining. Wrote it all out in Japanese first, then translated it to English. Except I used an online translator and didn't double-check."

"Oh no," Sofia said, already cringing.

"Instead of saying 'I think you're wonderful,' I told him 'I think you're a wonderful specimen.' Instead of 'I'd like to date you,' it came out as 'I'd like to data you.'" Yuki covered her face. "He thought I was asking to study him for a research project."

"What did he say?" Xu Fei asked.

"He offered to help me find 'better specimens' for my 'study.' I was too mortified to correct him. We spent the rest of the semester with him thinking I was conducting some kind of human behavior research."

The game continued, revelations flowing with the drinks. Louis told a story about getting lost in the Catacombs ("Terrible idea. Never follow someone who says they know a shortcut through an illegal entrance"). Yuki confessed to hating sushi ("I'm a disgrace to my nation"). Xu Fei admitted to having a secret Instagram account just for pictures of her neighbor's cat ("He's very photogenic"). Monique confessed to stealing her ex-husband's prized wine collection in the divorce ("He cried more about that than about losing me").

"Xu Fei," Isabella said. "Your turn. Truth—any romantic disasters we should know about?"

"Oh no," Xu Fei groaned. "Fine. Two years ago, I was dating this photographer. Very artistic, very sensitive. He decided to surprise me with a romantic gesture—filled my entire apartment with roses while I was at work."

"That sounds sweet," Yuki said.

"I'm severely allergic to roses. Ended up in the emergency room. He cried more than I did."

"Men and their feelings," Monique sighed. "So inconvenient when they have them."

"That's not fair," Louis protested. "We're allowed feelings."

"Of course you are, darling. Just have them quietly and without making them our problem."

"Okay, Louis," Hazel said, emboldened by wine and the memory of his hand in hers. "Truth. Why did you and Céleste break up?"

39

The question hung in the air between them like a challenge. Louis felt the table's attention shift, everyone suddenly very interested in their drinks while obviously listening.

"We dated for almost a year," he said, opting for honesty. Or at least a version of it. "Met at a gallery opening. She was brilliant, beautiful, everything you'd want. We talked about marriage, children, the whole future."

"What happened?" Hazel's voice was soft.

"I realized I was in love with the idea of her. The perfect life we'd have. But not actually her." He turned his whiskey glass, watching the amber liquid catch the light. "She deserved someone who loved her for who she was, not what she represented."

"That's very mature," Sofia said.

"We tried to be civilized about it. Mutual decision, stayed friends." He smiled wryly. "Though I suspect Céleste hid her frustration well. She's engaged now to someone who appreciates her properly. Even invited me to the wedding."

"Will you go?" Hazel asked.

He looked at her, really looked at her. Hair slightly mussed from the evening breeze, mascara smudged from laughing, absolutely nothing like Céleste's polished elegance. Absolutely perfect.

"Probably. Though I can't shake the feeling the invitation might be her very polite form of revenge."

"Right!" Yuki stood abruptly. "It's getting late. Xu Fei, shall we head back?"

"Already?" Isabella looked at her phone. "It's only—oh. It's midnight."

"One more stop!" Monique protested. "The night is young!"

"The night is middle-aged and has responsibilities," Sofia said, but she was already gathering her purse. "Though one more wouldn't hurt..."

They divided into camps—the clubbing trio determined to continue their evening, everyone else ready for bed. Louis watched Hazel yawn behind her hand and made the calculation.

"I'm heading back," he announced. "Share a taxi?"

"Please," Hazel said. "I've had enough excitement for one day."

"Lightweight," Isabella teased, but she was already pulling up a club on her phone. "We'll be good. Probably."

"Don't stay out too late," Louis warned. "You know how Chef Rousseau is with hangovers."

"Yes, dad," Monique said, rolling her eyes. "We'll be perfect angels."

The taxi ride passed in comfortable silence. Yuki dozed against Lu Fei's shoulder. Hazel stared out the window at Paris sliding by—lights and shadows and the occasional glimpse of the Seine. Louis found himself watching her reflection in the glass, the way the streetlights caught her profile. She looked thoughtful, maybe a little drunk, but definitely beautiful.

The villa was quiet when they arrived. Their footsteps echoed in the entrance hall as they climbed to the third floor. Yuki and Lu Fei peeled off first, whispering good nights. Then it was just Louis and Hazel, standing in the hallway between their doors.

"Today was fun," Hazel said. "Even the part where I almost got us arrested for art crimes."

"The statue had it coming. Very touchable. I blame the sculptor."

She laughed, then bit her lip. Louis watched her wrestle with something, saw the moment she made a decision.

She stepped into his space, rose up on her toes, and kissed him.

It was soft at first, tentative. Her lips tasted like wine and possibility. One hand rested lightly on his chest, the other curved around his neck. His hands found her waist automatically, steadying them both. The kiss deepened for just a moment—her mouth opening slightly under his, a tiny sound in her throat that made his pulse race—before she pulled back. Her eyes were bright, cheeks flushed.

"What was that for?"

"Today." She smiled, shy but sure. "And maybe tomorrow."

Her fingers traced down from his neck to his chest, leaving trails of fire even through his shirt. She was still close enough that he could feel her warmth, smell that light floral perfume mixed with wine and something uniquely her.

"If this is what I get for museum trips, I know exactly where we're going after class tomorrow."

"Maybe don't announce it to everyone this time?" Her smile turned teasing. "I'd like you to myself for once."

"Deal. Just us."

"Good night, Louis." She stepped back slowly, like she was reluctant to break the connection.

"Bonne nuit, Hazel."

She slipped into her room, glancing back once with a smile that made him lightheaded. Louis stood frozen in the hallway, heart hammering like he'd run a marathon. He could still taste the sweetness of her lips, feel the phantom pressure of her hand on his chest.

Louis touched his mouth, half-convinced he'd imagined it. But no. Hazel Chase, amateur detective and professional baker, had kissed him. The way she'd pressed against him, the little catch in her breathing—she wanted this as much as he did.

He let himself into his room, mind racing. Everything was getting complicated in ways he hadn't anticipated. But standing in his doorway, still feeling the ghost of her lips on his, he found he didn't care.

Whatever happened next, he couldn't mess this up. Not this. Not her.

40

The morning light filtered through the gauzy curtains, painting golden stripes across Hazel's rumpled sheets. She lay perfectly still, eyes closed, trying to hold onto the dream. Except it wasn't a dream. She'd actually done it. She'd kissed Louis Bassett in the hallway of a French villa at midnight like some character in one of her grandmother's romance novels.

Her fingers drifted to her lips. She could still feel the ghost of his mouth on hers, the way his hands had found her waist with such certainty. The tiny sound she'd made—God, had she really made that sound? Heat flooded her cheeks. She buried her face in the pillow, but the giddy smile wouldn't go away.

She'd kissed him. She, Hazel Chase, who'd never been particularly brave about anything except perfecting croissant dough, had stepped into his space and just... done it. The wine had helped, sure. Dutch courage, or French courage, or whatever you called it when you were in Paris. But the wine hadn't made her want to kiss him. That had been building for days.

The way he'd defended her at the bar, his hand finding hers so naturally. How he'd said "she's with someone" like it was the most obvious thing in the world. She'd replayed that moment approximately seventeen times before falling asleep.

And he'd kissed her back. Not politely, not out of surprise, but like he'd been waiting for it. The way his hands had tightened on her waist, pulling her closer for just that moment before she'd stepped away—

Stop it. She was twenty-five, not fifteen. She needed to get it together.

Her phone buzzed on the nightstand. WhatsApp notification. Her heart did a stupid little skip, thinking maybe Louis had messaged her. But it was just Xu Fei in the class group chat, excited about today's lesson and already planning camera angles. Hazel quickly checked her conversation with Mike—still just that lonely thumbs up emoji, unchanged since two nights ago.

For once, she didn't feel the familiar twist of impatience. Mike would find the woman when he found her. Right now, Hazel had more immediate concerns. Like what exactly last night's kiss meant. Were they dating now? Did one kiss in a hallway constitute dating? She'd never been good at reading these situations. Back home, relationships had been straightforward—you went to the movies a few times, maybe dinner at the one decent restaurant in town, and eventually someone asked "so are we official?" Usually over breadsticks at Olive Garden.

This felt different. Foreign in more ways than just the setting. She needed to look nice today. Better than nice. If they were going on an actual date—God, were they going on a date? He'd mentioned showing her something after class, just the two of them. That was a date, right?

She stumbled to the bathroom, catching sight of herself in the mirror. Her hair looked like she'd been electrocuted. Attractive. Very sexy. She'd definitely seduce Louis looking like she'd stuck her finger in a socket.

Shower first. Think later.

The hot water helped clear her head. She'd do something different with her hair. The same ponytail she'd worn every day wasn't going to cut it anymore. Not if she was dating Louis Bassett.

Dating. The word bounced around her head like a pinball.

She tried to remember the last time she'd put real effort into her appearance for a man. Tommy Park for prom, maybe? But that had been different. Expected. This was voluntary primping, which somehow felt more significant.

Her grandmother had taught her a few updos over the years, mostly for church events and the occasional wedding. There was one in particular—a twisted chignon with face-framing pieces—that Bridget had always said made Hazel look "like Grace Kelly, if Grace Kelly worked in a bakery."

It took three attempts and most of her travel-size hairspray, but finally she had something resembling the style. It changed her whole face, made her neck look longer, her cheekbones more defined. She looked... French. Or at least French-adjacent.

The knock came just as she was applying mascara for the second time (the first attempt had gone badly when she'd started thinking about Louis's hands in her hair).

"Un moment!" She grabbed her robe, made sure nothing inappropriate was showing, and opened the door.

Madame Dubois stood with the breakfast tray, her usual composed expression flickering for just a moment. Her eyes widened, focused on Hazel's hair, then darted away.

"Pardonnez-moi," the housekeeper said, regaining her composure so quickly Hazel wondered if she'd imagined the reaction. "You startled me, mademoiselle. With your hair like that, you reminded me of someone."

"Oh?" Hazel stepped back to let her in, curiosity piqued. "Who?"

Madame Dubois set the tray on the table with her usual efficiency, but her movements seemed stiffer than normal. "Just a woman who worked here once. Long time ago. She wore her hair in a similar style."

The words sent a tingle down Hazel's spine. "When was this? What was her name?"

"Marie. Marie Moreau." Madame Dubois adjusted the already-perfect placement of the coffee cup. "But that was many years ago. You enjoy your breakfast, yes?"

Marie. The name meant nothing to Hazel, but the timing... "Wait, Madame Dubois. This woman—Marie—did she know Charles?"

The housekeeper's face went carefully neutral. "Everyone knew Monsieur Lambert. He was the director."

"No, I mean—" Hazel's mind raced. Could it be? She grabbed her bag, pulling out the photograph. "Is this her?"

Madame Dubois took the frame with careful hands, studying the faces behind the glass. Her expression softened slightly, then hardened again.

"Non. This is not Marie." She looked up sharply. "Where did you get this photograph?"

The lie came easier than Hazel expected. "Charles gave it to me. Before he died. Those are my parents, in the middle. He said he knew them at university, but I never got to ask about the woman on the right. I was hoping to find her, see if she could tell me about them."

Madame Dubois looked at the photograph again, then handed it back. "It is definitely not Marie. And even if it were, I'm afraid you could not speak with her." She paused at the door, hand on the knob. "Marie is dead."

41

The words hung in the air like a physical presence. Hazel nearly dropped the photograph.

"Dead? What happened?"

Madame Dubois sighed, suddenly looking every one of her seventy-plus years. She glanced at the door as if checking for eavesdroppers, then stepped back into the room.

"You are a nice girl. You don't need to hear such sad stories."

"Please. I'd like to know."

Another sigh. Madame Dubois perched on the edge of the chair by the door, hands folded in her lap like a child in church.

"When the school first opened, there were two housekeepers. Myself and Marie. She was young, perhaps thirty. Very beautiful. The kind of beauty that brings trouble."

Hazel sat on the bed, breakfast forgotten.

"Monsieur Lambert was... different then. Younger, of course. Full of charm and ambition. He noticed Marie immediately." Madame Dubois's mouth tightened. "I do not speak ill of the dead, but Monsieur Lambert had appetites. Many women came and went. Marie was different. She was married, had a young son. But that did not stop him."

"They had an affair?"

"I cannot say for certain. But I have eyes. I saw how she began to change. Happy woman became sad woman. Smiled less. Spoke less. Some days she came to work with..." Madame Dubois gestured vaguely. "Marks. She said she was clumsy, but I knew better."

Hazel's stomach turned. She thought of Charles at the banquet, urbane and charming, pouring wine and telling stories. Had that same man hurt Marie?

"One morning, she did not come to work. We learned later—" Madame Dubois crossed herself. "She took her own life. Pills, they said."

"Oh my God."

"That is not the worst." Madame Dubois's voice dropped. "Her husband, he could not bear it. One month later, he too was gone. Jumped from a bridge into the Seine. Their son, ten or eleven years old, was left with nothing. No parents, no money, no home. The grandparents took him, I heard. I often wondered what became of that poor boy."

The room seemed to tilt. Hazel gripped the edge of the bed.

"Ten or eleven? When... when did this happen?"

"Fifteen years ago, perhaps. When the school was new." Madame Dubois stood, smoothing her black dress. "I should not have told you this. The past should stay buried with the dead."

"Thank you for telling me."

Madame Dubois paused at the door. "Enjoy your breakfast, mademoiselle. And perhaps... perhaps change your hair. The past has a way of haunting us when we look too much like it."

The door clicked shut. Hazel sat frozen, mind racing.

Louis's parents died when he was eleven. He'd said so that first day in the kitchen. His grandparents raised him—he'd mentioned that too.

No. She was being paranoid. Connecting dots that weren't there. Tragedy struck families everywhere—it didn't mean every orphaned child was connected to her story. And the name Marie Moreau meant nothing—it was probably as common as Mary Smith.

But the timeline fit perfectly. Fifteen years ago, Louis would have been eleven. The right age for Marie's son. And if Charles had driven Marie to suicide, if her death had triggered her husband's...

A boy that age would understand. Would see his mother coming home sad, hurt. Would hear her crying, maybe hear Charles's name. Would blame him when she died.

Would want revenge.

Hazel's hands shook as she poured coffee. The cup rattled against the saucer, brown liquid sloshing dangerously close to the rim.

If Louis was Marie's son—and that was a massive if—then he'd lied about everything. The investment story, the casual enrollment in the course. He'd come here for one reason: to kill Charles Lambert.

Which meant Priya was innocent. Sitting in a cell for a crime she didn't commit, tormented by blackouts and missing memories while the real killer made croissants and took Hazel to museums.

While the real killer kissed her in dark hallways.

No. She was jumping to conclusions based on coincidence and conjecture. She needed to calm down, think rationally. Just because the pieces fit didn't mean they belonged to the same puzzle.

But they did fit. Perfectly. Like ingredients measured precisely for a recipe that could only produce one result.

Hazel looked at her reflection in the mirror. The elaborate hairstyle that had made her feel sophisticated now made her look like a stranger. Like someone from the past bleeding into the present.

She pulled out the pins one by one, letting her hair fall back to its natural state. Safer this way. Less like Marie. Less likely to trigger memories in anyone who might have known her.

In anyone named Louis Bassett.

Her phone buzzed. A message in the class WhatsApp group from Eleanor: *Demonstration kitchen in thirty minutes. We're making Paris-Brest today!*

Thirty minutes to pull herself together. To face Louis and pretend everything was normal while her mind screamed questions. To stand next to him making pastry while wondering if his hands had held the dagger that killed Charles.

Those same hands that had held her last night. That had pulled her closer when she kissed him.

Hazel pressed her palms against her eyes, trying to stop the spinning in her head. She was probably wrong. Had to be wrong. The Louis she knew—funny, self-deprecating, kind—couldn't be a calculated killer who'd spent fifteen years planning revenge.

Could he?

42

Louis checked his watch for the third time in as many minutes. 8:57. The demonstration kitchen hummed with pre-class chatter, but he barely heard it. His eyes stayed fixed on the door, waiting.

Last night played on repeat in his mind. The softness of Hazel's lips, the way she'd pressed against him for just that moment, the little sound she'd made. He'd lain awake for hours afterward, replaying every second, every touch.

He should have kissed her first. Should have been braver, taken the lead instead of letting her make the first move. But then again, the fact that she had initiated it meant something. She'd wanted it as much as he had.

Today he'd take her to his favorite restaurant, the tiny place near the Madeleine church that tourists never found. Then the Ferris wheel at the Tuileries Garden just as the sun set, all of Paris spread out beneath them like a promise. It would be perfect. She deserved perfect.

The door opened. Louis straightened, then smiled.

Hazel walked in wearing her usual class outfit—worn jeans and a t-shirt that had seen better days. But something was different about her today. Maybe it was the way the morning light caught her face, or the careful way she moved, but she looked more beautiful than he'd ever seen her.

"Morning," Hazel said, not quite meeting his eyes.

"You look beautiful." The words came out without thought, sincere and too revealing. "I mean—good morning. Sleep well?"

"Fine." She busied herself with her apron, fingers fumbling the ties. "You?"

"Like a baby." A lie. He'd barely slept, too keyed up from their kiss, too excited about today. "Everything alright?"

She glanced up, and something in her expression made his chest tighten. She looked... wary? Distant? Not like a woman who'd kissed him eight hours ago.

"Everything's fine." But her smile didn't reach her eyes. "Looking forward to tonight?"

"More than you know." He moved closer, lowering his voice. "I know this perfect restaurant. Tiny place, only eight tables. The chef trained under—"

"Sounds wonderful." She turned away to gather ingredients, effectively ending the conversation.

Louis stood there, wrong-footed and confused. Had he misread last night? No, she'd definitely wanted to kiss him. Had been the one to initiate it. But now she seemed to be building walls between them with every gesture.

Chef Rousseau burst in with his usual theatrical entrance, saving Louis from further awkwardness. "Today, we make Paris-Brest! Very complicated! You will cry tears of joy when you succeed!"

The class proceeded with its usual chaos. Isabella somehow managed to spray cream filling across three stations. Xu Fei documented every disaster for her millions of followers. But Louis barely noticed. His attention stayed fixed on Hazel, who worked with mechanical precision, barely speaking except to answer direct questions.

When their hands accidentally touched reaching for the same pastry bag, she jerked back like she'd been burned.

"Did I do something wrong?" he asked quietly while Chef Rousseau was distracted by Monique's attempts to pipe choux.

"No." But she still wouldn't look at him. "I'm just tired."

Tired. Right. The universal excuse for when someone didn't want to talk about what was really wrong.

Lunch was torture. Hazel sat at the far end of the table, flanked by Xu Fei and Sofia, actively participating in their conversation about Swedish customs. Louis tried to catch her eye several times, but she seemed fascinated by her bouillabaisse.

By the time they left for their date—and it was definitely a date, despite Hazel's strange mood—Louis was thoroughly confused. She'd dressed up, clearly made an effort with her appearance. The dress was new, or at least new to him, and she'd done something subtle with her makeup that made her eyes look brighter, more defined.

But she might as well have been a million miles away.

The restaurant was everything he'd promised. Intimate, candlelit, the kind of place where Parisians proposed and tourists never found. The owner greeted Louis by name, showed them to the best table by the window. The wine was perfect, the food exquisite.

Hazel smiled and nodded and said all the right things. But behind her eyes, Louis could see her mind working, churning through thoughts she wouldn't share.

"The fish is incredible," she said, cutting a precise bite.

"André is a master." Louis watched her chew, swallow, reach for her wine. Every movement seemed calculated. "Hazel, talk to me. What's wrong?"

"Nothing's wrong."

"You've barely looked at me all day. Last night you—" He stopped, not wanting to sound desperate. "I thought we had something."

"We do." Finally, she met his eyes. "I'm sorry. I'm being weird. It's just... a lot to process."

"The kiss?"

"Everything." She took a larger sip of wine. "Being here, the course, Charles, you..."

"Me?"

"Us. Whatever this is." She gestured between them. "I'm not good at this stuff. Dating. Relationships. Reading signals."

Some of the tension in his chest eased. "You seemed pretty good at it last night."

That got a real smile, small but genuine. "Dutch courage."

"French courage."

"That too."

They finished dinner in slightly warmer silence. Louis paid, waving away her protests, and led her back onto the street. The evening was perfect—warm but not hot, the sky turning purple at the edges.

"I want to show you something," he said, taking her hand. She let him, which felt like progress. "Trust me?"

"Okay."

The Ferris wheel at the Tuileries Garden rose above the city like a giant clock, its lights just beginning to twinkle in the growing dusk. The line was manageable—tourists were still at dinner—and soon they were climbing into a glass-enclosed pod.

Paris spread out beneath them as they rose, the city transforming into a carpet of lights. The Eiffel Tower dominated the horizon, already sparkling with its hourly light show. The Seine wound between buildings like a golden ribbon.

"It's beautiful," Hazel breathed, face pressed to the glass.

"Wait until we reach the top."

Higher and higher they climbed, the pod swaying gently. Other passengers pointed and took photos, but Louis only watched Hazel. The setting sun painted her skin gold, caught the hints of red in her hair.

At the apex, Paris lay conquered at their feet. The entire city seemed to pulse with life, with possibility. The perfect moment for what he'd planned.

Louis moved closer, reaching for her hand. Time to take the initiative, to kiss her properly without hallway shadows. To show her how he really felt.

She pulled her hand back.

"Hazel?"

She was looking at him with that same wary expression from the morning. But now there was something else. Fear? Suspicion?

"What's going on?" The words came out sharper than intended. "You've been strange all day. If you regret last night, just tell me. I'm a big boy, I can handle rejection."

"It's not that." She wrapped her arms around herself despite the warm evening. "The view is beautiful. The restaurant was perfect. You've been perfect. But—"

"But?"

She turned to face him fully, and the look in her eyes made his stomach drop.

"Does the name Marie Moreau mean anything to you?"

The world tilted. Louis gripped the rail of the pod, suddenly dizzy from more than height. He could lie. Make up some story, deflect and distract. He was good at that.

But looking at Hazel's face—beautiful, worried, already knowing—he found he was tired of lies.

"Yes," he said quietly. "That was my mother's name."

43

Hazel's heart hammered against her ribs. She'd been right. All the pieces, all the connections—she'd been right. She was trapped in a glass pod hundreds of feet above Paris with a murderer.

But Louis didn't look dangerous. He looked... defeated. Shoulders slumped, hands loose at his sides, like all the fight had drained out of him the moment she'd said his mother's name.

"Madame Dubois told me," Hazel said, surprised her voice came out steady. "About Marie. About what happened to her. And your father."

"Ah." He turned to look out at the city, profile etched against the lights. "I wondered how long before someone made the connection. Should have known it would be you. You notice everything."

"Is that why you're here? At the school?" She had to ask, even though she already knew. "Did you come here to kill Charles?"

The pod continued its slow descent. Through the glass walls, Hazel could see the other pods around them—a child pressing sticky hands against glass in one, a couple taking selfies in another, tourists pointing at the Eiffel Tower in a third. Normal people having normal experiences while Hazel's world tilted off its axis.

"Yes," Louis said finally. The single word hung between them like a blade.

She should be terrified. Should be calculating how to escape when they reached the ground, whether she could signal the operator, if anyone would help if she screamed. Instead, she felt a strange calm settle over her. He'd admitted it. No more lies, no more wondering. Just truth, however terrible.

"You killed Charles."

"Yes."

The pod lurched gently, continuing its circle. They were descending now, Paris rising to meet them. Still time. Still trapped in this bubble of confession.

"Tell me." She was surprised to find she meant it. "I need to understand."

Louis laughed, short and bitter. "Understand what? That I'm a monster? That I spent fifteen years planning revenge on a man who destroyed my family?"

"You're not a monster." The words came without thought, but she realized they were true. Monsters didn't look like they wanted to cry. Monsters didn't slump against Ferris wheel walls like the weight of their secrets was crushing them.

"You don't know what I've done."

"So tell me."

He studied her face for a long moment. Around them, Paris glittered and pulsed, oblivious to the small dramas playing out in its shadows.

"We weren't rich," he began. "That was another lie. My father worked construction when he could find it. My mother couldn't get decent work—no connections, no education beyond secondary school. We lived in a two-room flat in Belleville. Not the trendy Belleville of now. The Belleville where you barred your windows and didn't go out after dark."

The pod rose again, starting another rotation. Hazel said nothing, afraid to break the spell of his confession.

"When Maman got the job at the pastry school, it felt like winning the lottery. Steady work, good pay, prestigious address. She'd clean up after rich students and come home with stories about soufflés that cost more than our weekly groceries." His mouth twisted. "She was so happy. At first."

"What changed?"

"Charles noticed her." The name came out like poison. "Beautiful Marie, too pretty to be pushing a mop. He had a way of making it seem like kindness, you know? Extra pay for extra tasks. Stay late to help with inventory. Special projects that required them to work closely together."

Hazel thought of Charles at the banquet, charming and paternal. How easily charm could mask darker appetites.

"She started coming home later. Quieter. The stories stopped." Louis's hands clenched on the rail. "I was eleven, but I wasn't stupid. I saw the bruises she tried to hide. Heard her crying when she thought I was asleep. Heard his name when she had nightmares."

"Did she tell you what was happening?"

"She didn't have to. I knew she couldn't quit—we needed the money. I knew she was trapped. And I knew it was killing her, day by day, like watching someone drown in slow motion."

The pod reached its apex again. The whole city spread beneath them, beautiful and indifferent.

"The night she died, she made my favorite dinner. Helped me with homework. Papa was working a construction job in Lille, staying overnight like he sometimes did for the better money. Everything seemed perfectly normal. She kissed me goodnight and told me she loved me, but there was something about the way she held me. Like she was saying goodbye." His voice broke slightly. "I found her the next morning. The pills were still on her nightstand."

"Oh, Louis."

"Papa tried. He really tried. But without her…" Louis shrugged, a fundamentally French gesture that somehow contained infinite sadness. "One month later, he jumped from a bridge into the Seine early in the morning. They found his body the next day."

Hazel wanted to reach for him but didn't know if she should. If comfort from her would help or hurt.

"My grandparents took me in. Good people, simple people. They didn't understand why their son was dead, why their daughter-in-law had left them a broken grandchild. I couldn't tell them. How do you explain that kind of evil to people who've never encountered it?"

"So you planned revenge."

"Not at first. At first I just wanted to die too. Eleven years old and already done with the world." He smiled without humor. "But dying felt like letting him win. Letting Charles continue his life while my parents rotted in the ground. So I decided to live. To grow up. To make him pay."

"Was the inheritance story a lie too? The money from your grandparents?"

"Complete lie. The truth is even more unbelievable." He laughed shortly. "When I was thirteen, I read an article about this new thing called Bitcoin. Digital currency, the article said. The future of money. I invested all my saved pocket money—birthday gifts, euros scraped together from odd jobs. By the time I was twenty-one, I was rich enough to disappear."

"And university? You mentioned both Oxford and Sorbonne..."

"Sorbonne was real. Oxford was..." He looked embarrassed. "I wanted to impress you. Thought it sounded better. But yes, I went to Sorbonne. Learned to speak like the elite, dress like them, move through their world like I belonged."

"All to get to Charles."

"I studied him for years. Every article, every interview. Learned his routines, his weaknesses. The school was perfect—contained environment, limited suspects, plausible reason for being there." He turned to face her. "I never expected you."

The words hit her like a physical blow. "Me?"

"You were supposed to be background. Another rich dilettante playing at pastry. Instead you were..." He gestured helplessly. "You. Funny and kind and terrible at lying and absolutely nothing like anyone I'd ever met. When you found Charles's body, the way you shook in my arms—I wanted to tell you everything. Wanted to confess just so you'd stop looking so scared."

"But you didn't."

"I'm very good at wanting things I shouldn't have." His smile was self-mocking. "Story of my life, really. Wanted parents who didn't die. Wanted revenge on a man who probably never thought twice about the housekeeper he destroyed. Wanted you even though I knew it would end like this."

The pod descended again, but this time Hazel found herself wishing it would slow down. She needed more time, needed to hear everything before they returned to solid ground where confessions had consequences and truths demanded action.

"The night of the murder," Hazel said. "Tell me what really happened."

Louis sighed, seeming to age a decade in seconds. "Do you really want to know?"

She thought of Priya in a cell, tormented by blackouts and guilt. Thought of Charles bleeding out in his office, taking secrets about her parents to his grave. Thought of Louis's lips on hers, his hands on her waist, all of it built on lies.

"Yes. I need to know everything."

44

The Night of the Murder

Louis stood outside Yuki's door, listening to her breathing deepen into sleep. Finally. He'd spent the last ten minutes helping her navigate the stairs, steadying her when she swayed, easing her onto the bed when her legs gave out. She'd mumbled something in Japanese before passing out, still in her dress and shoes.

The hallway stretched before him, dimly lit by sconces turned low for the night. Third floor of a Parisian villa, all elegant woodwork and worn runners that did little to muffle sound. He moved down the stairs, pausing halfway when he heard voices.

Voices. Coming from the second floor.

"—put that dagger back and let's have a normal conversation." Charles's voice, tight with controlled anger.

"Normal?" Priya's voice cracked. "Nothing about this is normal. You promised—"

"I promised to consider your proposal. I've considered it. The answer is no."

"You bastard. You absolute—"

A door slammed. Footsteps pounded up the stairs. Louis pressed himself against the wall, melting into shadow as Priya rushed past. Her face was flushed, eyes bright with unshed tears. She didn't see him. Too focused on her rage, probably.

He waited until her footsteps faded on the floor above. Then he assessed.

Isabella, Monique, and Sofia had left for the clubs, giggling like teenagers. Eleanor had gone to bed early, complaining about jet lag. Yuki was passed out. Hazel and Xu Fei were still in the dining room, probably discussing tomorrow's lesson. Madame Dubois and the kitchen staff were cleaning up after the banquet. Priya had just stormed off to her room.

Which meant Charles was alone in his office. With a dagger he'd just mentioned.

Louis's hand drifted to his pocket, fingers finding the latex glove he'd carried for days. Just in case.

Fifteen years he'd waited for this moment. Fifteen years of planning, of building himself into someone who could get close to Charles Lambert. Rich enough to afford the course. Charming enough to blend in. Patient enough to wait for the perfect opportunity.

And here it was, delivered like a gift.

He moved down the stairs, each step measured. The second-floor hallway was darker than the third. Only one sconce still glowed. Charles's office door stood slightly ajar, a slice of light cutting across the Persian runner.

Louis paused outside, listening. The scratch of a pen. A heavy sigh. The clink of glass—Charles pouring himself another drink.

He knocked softly.

"Come in." Charles sounded tired. Older than his fifty years.

Louis pushed the door open, stepped inside. The office was exactly what he'd expected. Leather and mahogany, awards on the walls, the smell of expensive wine and cigars. Charles sat behind his desk, a half-empty glass of red wine at his elbow. The ceremonial dagger lay near the edge of the desk, its jeweled handle catching the light.

Charles looked up, eyebrows rising slightly. "Louis. Rather late for a social call."

"I couldn't sleep." Louis closed the door behind him, leaning against it. "Thought I might find you here."

"Insomnia loves company." Charles gestured to a chair. "Sit. Drink?"

"No, thank you."

Charles studied him over the rim of his glass. Those sharp eyes that missed nothing, or at least thought they didn't. "You're not really here to fulfill some New Year's resolution, are you?"

Louis smiled. Not his charming smile, the one that made women flutter. This was different. Colder. "Clever man."

"I've been running this school for fifteen years. I know when someone's playing a role." Charles set down his glass carefully. "So who are you really?"

"My name really is Louis Bassett, if that's what you're asking." He pulled the glove from his pocket, began working it onto his right hand. Slowly. No rush now. "But you might remember my mother better. Marie Moreau."

The color drained from Charles's face. The glass trembled in his hand.

"Marie." The name came out as a whisper. "My God. You're Marie's boy."

"I was eleven when she killed herself." Louis finished with the glove, flexing his fingers. The latex made a soft snapping sound. "Eleven years old, trying to understand why Maman would swallow a bottle of pills. Why she'd leave me alone."

Charles's hand moved toward the dagger. Louis was faster, his hand closing over the jeweled handle.

"Don't." Louis lifted the blade, testing its weight. Good balance. Sharp enough to slice paper. "We're going to talk first. You're going to tell me you remember her."

"Of course I remember her." Charles's voice was steady now. Resigned. "Beautiful Marie. Too beautiful for her own good."

"Too beautiful for a housekeeper, you mean. Too beautiful to leave alone."

Charles closed his eyes. "I was different then. Young. Stupid. I thought—" He stopped, shook his head. "No. No excuses. I hurt her. I know that."

"Hurt her?" Louis laughed, but there was no humor in it. "You destroyed her."

"I was wrong." Charles opened his eyes, meeting Louis's gaze directly. "I've regretted it every day since. When I heard about... about what she did... I wanted to die myself."

"But you didn't. You lived. You thrived. Built this prestigious school on the ashes of the people you crushed." Louis moved closer, the dagger loose in his hand. "While I grew up without a mother. Without a father—did you know that? He jumped into the Seine a month after she died. Couldn't live without her."

"I didn't know." Charles's voice was barely audible. "Louis, I'm so—"

"Don't." The word came out sharp as the blade. "Don't you dare apologize. Not now. Not after fifteen years."

Silence stretched between them, heavy as grief. Charles sat perfectly still, hands flat on the desk. No attempt to run. No pleas for mercy. Just waiting.

"You're probably wondering why I don't share my mother's surname," Louis said finally. "Moreau. She kept her maiden name when she married my father. Professional pride, she said. If you'd ever treated her as more than just another pretty thing in your school, you might have known that. Might have known she had a husband, a son, a whole life beyond your school."

"No," Charles admitted. "I never asked. I never... God, I was such a fool."

"Yes. You were." Louis gripped the dagger's handle tighter. "I've imagined this moment for fifteen years. What I'd say. What you'd say. How you'd beg."

"I won't beg." Charles reached for his glass, took a long swallow. "If you're going to do it, do it. I won't fight you. I've been running from my sins for fifteen years. Maybe it's time to stop."

Louis stared at him. This wasn't how it was supposed to go. Charles should be terrified. Should be offering money, connections, anything to save his worthless life. Not sitting there like some penitent waiting for absolution.

"You want to die?"

"Want?" Charles laughed bitterly. "No. But I understand why you're here. What I did to your mother... there's no forgiveness for that. No redemption. Just debt." He set down his glass, straightened his tie. "So collect your debt, Louis Bassett. Your mother's son. Take what you came for."

The dagger felt heavier now. Louis moved around the desk, standing close enough to smell Charles's cologne. Something expensive, with notes of sandalwood and regret.

"Any last words?"

Charles looked up at him. Those sharp eyes were calm now. Accepting. "Tell Eleanor the school should continue. Tell her... tell her I'm sorry for leaving such a mess."

"That's it? Nothing else?"

"What else is there? I can't undo the past. Can't bring Marie back. Can't give you back your childhood." Charles closed his eyes. "Just... make it quick. I'm tired of carrying this weight."

Louis raised the dagger. Fifteen years of planning, fifteen years of hate, fifteen years of grief—all distilled into this moment. His hand was steady. His breathing even.

He drove the blade into Charles's chest.

It went in easier than he'd expected. Through fabric and flesh, finding the spaces between ribs like it was designed for this purpose. Charles gasped, eyes flying open. His hands clutched at the jeweled handle, but Louis held it firm, pushing deeper.

Blood spread across Charles's white shirt. His mouth opened and closed, no words coming out. Just a soft wheeze, like air escaping a punctured tire.

Louis watched the life drain from those sharp eyes. Watched them go dull and fixed. Felt the moment when Charles Lambert stopped being a person and became just memory.

He'd expected to feel something. Satisfaction. Joy. Relief. Fifteen years of anticipation, and now... nothing. Just a dead man bleeding out on expensive leather and a hollowness in his chest that matched the hole he'd put in Charles.

Maybe because Charles hadn't been afraid. Hadn't begged or fought or done any of the things Louis had imagined. He'd just...

accepted it. Like he'd been waiting for someone to collect this particular debt.

The blood was spreading too fast, dripping onto the Persian rug. Louis pulled his hand back, leaving the dagger where it was. A monument to old sins and fresh revenge.

What now? Fifteen years of living for this moment, and he'd never thought much about what came after. He'd built his entire adult life around this plan. Went to the right schools, made the right connections, accumulated enough wealth to seem credible. All to get close enough to Charles Lambert to slide a blade between his ribs.

Mission accomplished. Now what?

Louis peeled off the glove, careful not to leave prints on anything. He tucked it into his pocket. The smart thing would be to leave immediately. Pack his things, disappear into the night. He had accounts in Switzerland, a flat in London no one knew about. He could vanish.

But vanishing now would point directly to him. The student who disappears right after a murder? Every police force in Europe would be hunting him within hours. Better to stay, play the shocked innocent, let the investigation run its course. He was good at playing roles. He'd been playing them his whole life.

Louis took one last look at Charles. The man who'd destroyed his mother looked smaller in death. Just an old man who'd made terrible choices and finally paid for them. Not the monster Louis had built up in his mind. Just a man.

He backed out of the office, pulling the door almost closed. Left it slightly ajar, the way he'd found it. Then he walked down the stairs, breathing normally.

The dining room doors were closed, but he could hear voices inside. Hazel's laugh, bright as champagne bubbles. Xu Fei's more reserved chuckle.

Louis straightened his cuffs, ran a hand through his hair. Time to put on the mask again. Time to be charming Louis Bassett, the slightly arrogant rich boy who'd enrolled in pastry school on a whim.

He pushed open the dining room doors, smile already in place.

45

The Ferris wheel pod touched down with a gentle bump, the ride operator already reaching for the safety bar. Sixty meters above Paris, and now they were back on solid ground. The whole story told in one revolution.

Hazel's legs felt unsteady as she stepped out. Not from the height or the movement, but from the weight of what she'd just heard. Louis followed, his hand briefly touching her elbow to steady her. She pulled away.

"Don't."

He dropped his hand immediately. Around them, the Tuileries Garden stretched out in manicured perfection, its paths lit by ornate lampposts. Tourists snapped photos of the giant wheel, temporary installation transforming the historic gardens into a glittering fairground. None of them knew they were walking past a confessed murderer.

"Why didn't you leave?" The question burst out before Hazel could stop it. "After you... after Charles died. Why stay?"

Louis started walking away from the wheel, and she found herself following despite everything. They needed distance from the crowds, from the bright lights that made every emotion visible.

"It would have looked suspicious." His voice was matter-of-fact, like they were discussing the weather. "The student who vanishes right after a murder? The police would have focused on me immediately. Better to stay, play the concerned friend, the shocked innocent."

"Is that all it was? Playing a role?"

He stopped walking, turned to face her. "At first, yes. But then you screamed, and I ran upstairs, and you were standing there shaking..." He shrugged, that fundamentally French gesture. "You looked so lost. I couldn't just leave you like that."

"How noble." The sarcasm tasted bitter. "The murderer with a heart of gold."

"I never claimed to be noble." They started walking again, moving away from the brightest lights. "But I'm not a monster, Hazel. I didn't enjoy it. Didn't feel the satisfaction I'd expected. Just... emptiness."

"Charles is still dead."

"Yes."

"And Priya's been in police custody for five days thinking she might have killed him during a blackout."

Louis's jaw tightened. "I never meant for anyone else to be blamed. When they arrested her, I thought about confessing. Almost did, twice. But—"

"But you're a coward."

"Yes." No defensiveness, just agreement. "I'm a coward who spent fifteen years planning revenge and then didn't know what to do with himself once it was done. And then there was you."

"Don't." Hazel's voice cracked. "Don't you dare make this about me."

"I'm not. I'm just explaining." He stopped again. "For fifteen years, my only purpose was revenge. Kill Charles Lambert. Make him pay for destroying my mother. I never thought about what came after because I couldn't imagine an after."

The Ferris wheel's lights illuminated his face. He looked young suddenly, despite being a year older than her. Young and lost and terribly sad.

"Then I met you," he continued. "This American baker who attacked pastry like it personally offended her. Who made jokes during the worst possible moments. Who kissed me in a dark hallway."

"If I'd known what you'd done, I never would have."

"No," he agreed. "Of course not."

They stood in silence, the city humming around them. Somewhere, church bells marked the half hour with a single chime. Half past nine. The August twilight was finally fading, but Paris was just coming alive—cafés still serving, lovers still strolling along the Seine.

"I can't forgive you," Hazel said finally. "Charles was going to tell me about my parents. You took that away from me."

"I know."

"He recognized me, Louis. He knew something about them, about why they died, about the money. And now I'll never find out."

"I'm sorry." The words sounded inadequate even to her. "If I'd known—"

"Would it have mattered? Really? Would you have let him live if you'd known he had information I needed?"

Louis was quiet for a long moment. "I don't know. I'd like to think so, but... I don't know."

At least he was honest. Small comfort, but she'd take what she could get.

"What happens now?" she asked.

"Now?" Louis looked at her with those amber eyes that had fooled her so completely. "Now I turn myself in. I tell that detective everything. Priya goes free. You finish your course and try to forget you ever met me."

"Just like that?"

"What else is there? I can't undo it. Can't bring Charles back. Can't give you the answers you need." He straightened, pulling his shoulders back. "But I can stop being a coward. I can own what I did."

He turned to go, then paused. "Goodbye, Hazel Chase. I hope you find what you're looking for. And I hope... I hope you find someone better than me. You deserve better than beautiful lies and ugly truths."

Louis walked away, heading back toward the Ferris wheel where uniformed officers patrolled. Tourist area, high security. He'd be arrested within minutes.

Hazel watched him go, this man she'd thought she was falling for. This murderer who'd charmed his way into her life. This broken boy who'd spent most of his life planning revenge for a mother he'd loved.

She waited until she saw him approach the officers, watched him hold out his wrists for the handcuffs. Then she walked in the opposite direction, letting the city swallow her whole.

46

The news had broken before the morning class. Detective Arnaud arriving with uniformed officers, gathering everyone in the entrance hall. The announcement delivered in that flat tone police used for shocking revelations. Louis Bassett had confessed to the murder of Charles Lambert. Priya Patel was released without charges. The investigation was closed.

Eleanor had swayed on her feet. Xu Fei had gasped. Yuki had muttered something in Japanese that didn't sound polite. The clubbing trio had clutched each other like survivors of a shipwreck.

And Hazel had stood there, playing shocked. Playing confused. Playing the betrayed almost-girlfriend who'd had no idea the charming Frenchman was capable of murder.

She was getting good at playing roles too.

A knock interrupted her brooding. "Come in."

Priya stood in the doorway, looking older than her thirty-five years. The past week had carved new lines around her eyes, turned her dark hair dull. But she was free. That was what mattered.

"I'm leaving for London in a few minutes," Priya said. "Decided to pack up and go home. But I wanted to say goodbye first. And thank you."

"For what?"

"For finding the truth." Priya stepped into the room, closing the door behind her. "I know you're the one who figured it out. Who made him confess."

Hazel shrugged. "I just asked questions."

"You did more than that." Priya sat on the edge of the bed, hands clasped in her lap. "I thought I was going mad. The blackouts, the missing memories, my earring in his office... I was so certain I'd killed him and blocked it out."

"Trauma can do that. Make you doubt yourself."

"Yes." Priya was quiet for a moment. "The truth is, I wanted to hurt him that night. When he rejected my offer, laughed at me for thinking I could poach his chef... I was furious. It turns out I actually picked up that dagger, held it in my hands. If I'd used it instead of putting it back..."

She didn't finish, but she didn't need to. Hazel understood. The thin line between thought and action, between anger and violence. How easy it was to cross when pushed.

"But you didn't," Hazel said. "That's what matters."

"Is it?" Priya looked at her directly. "Louis crossed that line. Whatever his reasons, however justified he felt, he took a life. He'll go to prison for that. Years of his life, gone. Was it worth it?"

Hazel thought about Louis's empty expression after the confession. The way he'd said he felt nothing after fifteen years of anticipation. "I don't think he thought it was."

"No. I suppose not." Priya stood, smoothing her skirt. "Are you staying? To finish the course?"

"Yeah. I paid a lot of money for this. Might as well learn something."

"Practical." Priya smiled slightly. "Well, good luck. And Hazel? Be careful who you trust. This world, these people with money and secrets... it's more dangerous than you think."

After Priya left, Hazel lay back on her bed. At least her amateur sleuthing had saved one innocent person from a wrongful conviction. That had to count for something.

Her phone buzzed. WhatsApp notification.

Her heart jumped—Mike?—but it was just Janet asking for updates. Hazel ignored it. She'd deal with Janet later, when she figured out how to explain that the cute French boy turned out to be a murderer.

Instead, she opened her photos, scrolling to the picture she'd taken of Charles's photograph. Four young people, bright with promise. Charles and her parents and the mystery woman. Her only lead now that Charles was gone.

She opened WhatsApp again, checking her chat with Mike. Still that single thumbs up emoji staring back. But wait—there was something new. Three dots. He was typing.

The dots disappeared. Appeared again. Disappeared.

"Come on," Hazel muttered. "Just send it."

As if he'd heard her, a message appeared. Not words—a link. She clicked it immediately.

Facebook profile. Vittoria Rossi, 49, Rome. Tour guide at the Colosseum. The profile picture was recent, but the face was unmistakable. The same woman from Charles's photograph, older now but still recognizable.

Hazel's hands shook as she typed: *Thank you.*

Mike responded with a single thumbs up emoji.

That was it. No words, no "you're welcome," just an emoji. But he hadn't blocked her this time. Progress, maybe. Perhaps their friendship could be salvaged after all.

She studied the Facebook profile. Vittoria's last post was two years old, something about renovations at the Colosseum. Since then, nothing. But she hadn't deactivated the account, which meant she might still check messages.

Hazel opened Messenger, staring at the blank composition box. How did you explain this? "Hi, you don't know me, but I think you knew my dead parents and I'm investigating their mysterious fortune and also I just solved a murder at a French pastry school and—"

Yeah, that would go well.

She started typing, deleting, typing again. Finally settled on simple:

Hello Vittoria. My name is Hazel Chase. I believe you knew my parents, Thomas and Olivia Chase. I recently found a photograph of you with them and Charles Lambert. I'm trying to understand some things about their death and would very much like to speak with you. I'm currently in Paris but could come to Rome if you're willing to meet. Please, any information would help. Thank you.

She hit send before she could overthink it further. Message delivered. Now all she could do was wait.

The villa felt too quiet. Everyone was probably in their rooms, processing the morning's revelations. How many would abandon the course now? How many would stay?

Hazel knew she would. Not because she particularly cared about pastry anymore—that dream felt distant now, like something a younger, more innocent version of herself had wanted. But because leaving felt like giving up.

Besides, she'd already learned so much. Not about baking, but about people. About how grief could twist into revenge. About how charm could mask darkness. About how anyone was capable of anything, given the right pressure.

Lessons you couldn't get from a cookbook.

47

The final certificate ceremony was subdued. Six students where there should have been eight, gathered in the dining room that had hosted that fatal banquet. Eleanor had insisted on pushing through, finishing what Charles had started. "He would have wanted the show to go on," she'd said, and no one had the heart to argue.

They'd had another week of classes after Louis's arrest. Chef Rousseau throwing himself into teaching with manic energy, as if perfect croissants could somehow make up for murder. The remaining students going through the motions, whisking and folding and baking on autopilot.

Hazel had partnered with Xu Fei, who turned out to be surprisingly funny when not filming everything. They'd made opera cake and mille-feuille and tarte tatin, each day a little less awkward than the last. No one mentioned Louis. No one mentioned Charles. They baked and learned and pretended everything was normal.

Now Eleanor stood at the head of the table, holding a stack of certificates. She wore black, as she had every day since Charles's death. It aged her, made her look like she was attending a funeral that never ended.

"I want to thank you all," Eleanor began, her voice carefully steady. "For staying. For persevering through... difficult circumstances. Charles built this school on the belief that art could transcend tragedy. That beauty could emerge from pain. You've all proven him right."

Madame Dubois stood by the door, hands clasped, watching with those sharp eyes that missed nothing. Chef Rousseau flanked Eleanor's other side, his usual exuberance dampened but not extinguished. Even Chef Bernard had emerged from his kitchen domain, still in his whites, hat slightly askew.

"Isabella Giuliani," Eleanor called.

Isabella stepped forward, still elegant despite the dark circles under her eyes. The past two weeks had taken their toll on everyone in different ways.

"Your passion for learning inspired us all," Eleanor said, handing over the certificate.

One by one, they went up. Monique, who'd developed a nervous laugh. Sofia, who'd started carrying a flask in her purse. Yuki, who'd switched from champagne to coffee, lots of coffee.

"Xu Fei," Eleanor called. "Your photos and videos of our school have reached thousands of viewers online. You've brought our work to the attention of aspiring pastry chefs across China and beyond."

Xu Fei accepted her certificate with a bow.

"Hazel Chase."

Hazel walked forward on unsteady legs. Eleanor's eyes were kind but knowing. How much did she suspect? How much did any of them suspect?

"You showed remarkable resilience," Eleanor said quietly, pressing the certificate into Hazel's hands. "Charles mentioned you specifically that last night. Said you had promise."

Hazel's throat closed up. "Thank you."

"No. Thank you." Eleanor squeezed her hands. "For everything."

The words carried weight, meaning beyond the simple exchange. Hazel nodded, not trusting her voice.

After the certificates, Chef Bernard's asssitants served a final meal. Not the elaborate banquet of that first night, but simple, perfect dishes. Coq au vin that melted on the tongue. Potatoes so creamy they defied physics. A chocolate soufflé that tasted like childhood dreams.

They ate quietly. Madame Dubois poured wine with a generous hand. Chef Rousseau told gentle stories about Charles's early days, painting a picture of an ambitious young chef before success and secrets complicated everything.

"What will happen to the school?" Hazel asked during a lull.

Eleanor set down her wine glass carefully. "I'm not sure. Charles left things... complicated. There are investors to consider, contracts to review. I think I'll close for a month or two. Take time to..." She waved vaguely. "Process. Grieve. Decide."

"It would be a shame to close permanently," Sofia said. "Despite everything, this is a special place."

"Yes." Eleanor's smile was sad. "Charles poured his heart into every stone. It would be wrong to let it die with him."

They toasted, crystal chiming against crystal. Outside, dusk painted the garden purple and gold. Hazel thought about Louis in a cell somewhere, about Priya rebuilding her life in London, about Charles bleeding out on Italian leather. About parents who died with secrets and fortunes that came from nowhere.

"I should pack," Yuki said finally, breaking the spell. "Early flight tomorrow."

The gathering dissolved slowly, everyone murmuring about flights and trains and lives waiting to resume. Hazel helped clear plates, needing something to do with her hands.

"Where will you go?" Xu Fei asked, stacking dishes. "Back to California?"

"I'm not sure." Hazel had been avoiding the question all week. "Maybe travel a bit first. See more of Europe while I'm here."

"If you come to Beijing, I'll show you real pastry. French technique, Chinese flavors. You'll love the fusion."

They hugged goodbye, promising to stay in touch. Empty promises probably, but comfort in the moment.

Eleanor caught Hazel at the stairs. "A word?"

They walked to the garden, now empty of students. The roses perfumed the air with their heavy scent. Somewhere in the distance, church bells marked the hour.

"I know what you did," Eleanor said without preamble. "I don't know how, exactly, but I know you're the reason Louis confessed. The reason Priya is free."

Hazel said nothing. Denial seemed pointless.

"Charles saw something in you," Eleanor continued. "That first night, he pulled me aside. Said you looked like someone he used to know. Said it was uncanny."

"Did he say who?"

"No. But he was shaken. Charles didn't shake easily." Eleanor turned to face her. "Whatever you're looking for, whatever brought you here... be careful. Charles kept secrets for a reason. Some doors are better left closed."

"Maybe. But I need to know."

Eleanor nodded slowly. "I understand. Just... remember that the dead keep their secrets for a reason. And sometimes the living pay the price for disturbing them."

She left Hazel alone in the garden, surrounded by roses and shadows. The villa glowed before her, windows warm with light. Tomorrow it would be empty, just Eleanor and the ghosts.

But tonight, it still held life. Complicated, messy, human life.

Hazel went to pack.

48

Her room looked strange, stripped of personal touches. Just expensive furniture and someone else's taste in art. Hazel folded clothes mechanically, trying not to think about Louis helping her with the tart, about that kiss in the hallway just outside this door, about Charles promising to tell her everything.

Two weeks in Paris. She'd learned to make perfect choux pastry and solve a murder. Not bad for a baker from Fillmore.

Her phone buzzed. She grabbed it eagerly—maybe Vittoria had responded?

But it was just the Facebook app notifying her that Kelly from high school had posted a new photo. Her message to Vittoria remained unanswered.

Hazel sat on the bed, suddenly exhausted. What was she doing? Chasing ghosts across Europe, looking for answers that might not exist. Her parents were dead. Had been for twenty-three years. Whatever secrets they'd carried had died with them.

Except.

Except for the money that had appeared from nowhere. Except for Charles's recognition. Except for a photograph of four young people who'd clearly meant something to each other.

Except for Vittoria Rossi in Rome, who'd read her message and chosen not to respond.

Hazel opened her laptop, searching for flights to Rome. If Vittoria wouldn't answer messages, maybe she'd answer the door. It was a long shot, but what else did she have? Go back to Fillmore with nothing but a pastry certificate and a story too wild to tell?

Flights from Paris to Rome were surprisingly cheap. She could leave tomorrow. Find a hotel near the Colosseum, stake out the tourist entrances until she spotted Vittoria. Tour guides had regular routes, regular schedules. It might take days, but Hazel had nothing but time now.

And money. Strange to think that was no longer a concern. She could stay in Europe for months if needed, following every lead, turning over every stone. Her grandmother's—her parents'—fortune making it all possible.

She booked the flight. Tomorrow, 3 PM. Paris to Rome in two hours. By dinner time, she'd be in the Eternal City, hunting for a woman who might hold the key to everything.

The End
... of the first book in the series

Author's Note

Thank you so much for reading this book! I hope you had as much fun getting to know Hazel and exploring Paris with her as I did writing it.

This is just the beginning of her story. Hazel still has a long way to go as she travels across Europe, chasing down the truth about her parents. I know you're probably dying to know what really happened to them and where that money came from. Can I tell you a secret? I'm still figuring it out myself. We'll discover the answers together as Hazel's journey continues.

I tried my best to bring the real Paris to life in these pages, though I'll confess I bent the truth a bit when the story needed it. That's the beauty of fiction, right? Just a heads up—I'll probably do the same thing with the other European cities in the series.

If you enjoyed the book, I'd really appreciate it if you could leave a review on Amazon or Goodreads—or both, if you're up for it. I genuinely read every single one, and your feedback means the world to me.

Want to be the first to know about new releases and updates? Sign up for my newsletter, and as a thank you, you'll receive a FREE exclusive short story: *"Takedown in Fillmore."* It reveals how Hazel went from the worst student in her self-defense class to defeating her longtime rival—a fun glimpse into her teenage years in Fillmore that I wrote just for my newsletter subscribers.

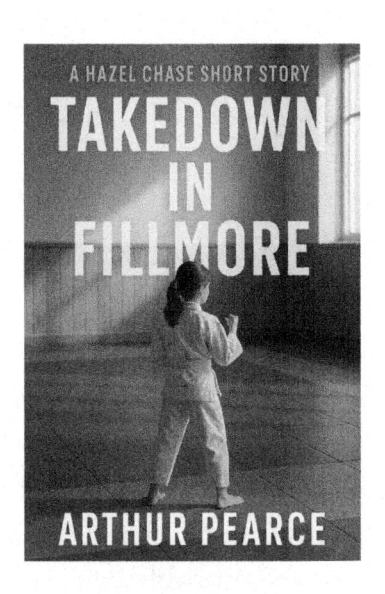

https://www.arthurpearce.com/newsletter

Thanks again for coming along on this journey with Hazel and me. See you in the next city!

Hazel's Story Continues

What secrets does Vittoria Rossi hold?
Find out in *Murder in Rome*!

Coming *October 10, 2025*

Also by Arthur Pearce

Jim and Ginger Cozy Mysteries
A retired librarian and his cat solve mysteries in a coastal town

Printed in Dunstable, United Kingdom